James Philip

EMPIRE DAY

The New England Series – Book 1

Cover concept by James Philip
Graphic Design by Beastleigh Web Design

———————

Contents

ACT I – THE DAY BEFORE

Saturday 3rd July 1976

Chapter 1

Gravesend, King's County, Long Island

It is a fact generally acknowledged that when a squad of heavily armed policeman and soldiers breaks down one's front door, drags one out of bed – ignoring the screams of one's wife; incidentally, I had no idea she could scream so loudly – and pins one to the floor with the muzzle of a gun to one's head that, all things considered, it is not wholly unreasonable to conclude that one is probably in a lot of trouble.

Things calmed down a little after the initial excitement.

'Isaac Putnam Fielding,' a plain clothes police officer had informed me, a little breathlessly, 'you are under arrest for suspicion of fomenting sedition.'

That had not happened lately.

What was it they said about variety being the spice of life?

I was hauled to my feet.

Sarah, my wife, had stopped screaming; we had only been married a year or so – well, in the common law sense of the term - but none of that ought to have come as much of a surprise. Our very common law 'marriage', I mean. She was twenty-eight years my junior, had been one of my graduate students and in the beginning at least, seemingly infatuated by my reputation for being one of, well, most of the time, the University's *only* surviving dissident from the old days. That had been the attraction: Sarah was bright, ambitious, angry – and as cute as Hell – a redhead with Irish green eyes who ought to have shacked up with somebody her own age and started a family by now. Instead, she had moved in with my much-diminished brood; or as my unwanted guests would say: former 'nest of seditious vipers'.

My father always used to say that the thing which really got his goat about the English was that they were always so 'goddammed polite'.

My midnight guests – actually, they had come through the front door at around one o'clock that morning – had apologised to Sarah once she stopped screaming, whom a female officer had quickly guided out of the bedroom of our big old white boarded house on the rising ground on Howe Street overlooking Gravesend Bay. Then they suggested to me that I should get dressed.

'Do I need my courtroom rig?' I had inquired, without irony. This shit had not happened to me for a while but I remembered 'the form'. If I got hauled up in front of a magistrate there would be photographers outside and sketch artists inside the chamber; one wanted to look one's best for one's public on TV and in the papers.

'Casual is good,' the senior cop grunted.

Everything had settled down now although I could hear methodical movement all over the house. These people were from Manhattan, the locals would have crashed about like a herd of stampeding Bison.

Two men stayed with me as I got dressed.

Slacks, a chequered shirt – twenty years ago I would have said 'to hide the blood' – but that was then and this was now;

the rough stuff was over for the minute and the Governor of the twin-colony, formerly a High Court Judge back in the old country, took a dim view of his officials beating up on suspects. I pulled on open-toed sandals - this was going to be a long day and I might as well be comfortable - and nodded to the wardrobe before picking out an old jacket with leather elbow pads.

The cops patted down my pockets.

We all knew the drill.

These raids had been much more traumatic while Rachel had still been alive and the kids had been younger. I had got older, complacent, and Abe apart the kids had completely cut the parental umbilical cord and moved out for good.

Not that my youngest boy spent much time at home these days. He was up at college in Albany, a fourth and final-year medical student. Abe did not get on with Sarah, and basically, he only came home to catch up with his boyhood friends on high days and holidays.

I pulled on my jacket and held out my wrists.

The handcuffs clicked.

"That okay," the younger of the two cops asked solicitously.

I flexed my hands.

"Yeah, that's a good fit, son."

The older of my visitors showed me his warrant card.

Detective Inspector M.R.D. Danson.

He was my age, greying at the temples with watchful grey eyes and he had kept well out of the way while his people had jumped on me.

Special Branch...

"Do you know where your son is, sir?"

"Which one, Inspector?"

Danson indicated for his sidekick to leave the bedroom, pointed for me to sit on the bed while he pulled up the chair by Sarah's dresser and planted his obviously weary bones on it about a yard away from me.

"You know how this works, Professor," he sighed. "We've never met but I've seen your file. You and me, we're old school. We play the game, that way nobody really gets hurt. But what's going to happen when I take you to Hempstead is that my boys are going to tear this place apart looking for firearms and explosives…"

"Seriously?"

"I need to know where Abe is?" Danson asked quietly, his grey eyes suddenly boring into my face.

"Abe?" I felt as dumbfounded as I must have looked. We had got off lightly with Victoria, our eldest kid, but Alexander and his brother William had both gone through phases when Rachel and I had got so fed up having the local constabulary calling we had, very nearly, thought better of our vow never to lay an angry hand upon any of our offspring.

Victoria had married a widower and lived in fashionable Clintonville on the north shore of Long Island. I did not get to see my two grandchildren very often; Vicky was probably afraid I would corrupt their innocent young minds. Her husband, John Watson, was a big man at the Brooklyn Admiralty Dockyard at Wallabout Bay, he was more or less my age but we had always got along civilly.

Alexander had gone into the twin-colonies militia straight out of school, learned to fly and led a harem-scarum life ever since. I had tried to get him to talk about his time flying scouts down in the South West; but like most veterans of the Border War he rarely spoke about what it was really like down there.

William, my middle boy, had become a *real* teenager after Alex went into the militia, moody, introspective and argumentative at the drop of a hat he had bummed out of school without matriculating, learned to be a mechanic doing his militia service 'in state' and these days worked for the Long Island Speedboat Company. So far as I knew he spent most of his free time at church – he had turned Puritan in recent years – because I had not seen him since the Christmas before last. We had had words and the sanctimonious little runt had not shown his face in Gravesend since. I ought to have felt worse about that but actually it was a relief.

But Abe...

Abe was our accidental fourth child, by six-and-a-half years the youngest, the baby of the family who had grown up to be the tallest, and by far and away the brightest addition to the Fielding brood.

Abe was the gentlest boy in the neighbourhood, bookish, shy as a kid behind his spectacles – he was a little short-sighted as a child, a thing he had grown out of – the sort of kid the girls tried to protect in the playground. Heck, the colonial militia had turned him down for service on account of his 'eye history' when he was eighteen, and that alleged brush he had had with rheumatic fever – which Rachel had had conveniently documented in advance - as a kid. Heck, Rachel was never going to let her third son get drafted without a fight...

"Abe?" I repeated, wondering if I had misheard. "Abe's up at Albany studying..."

"At medical school, I know," the detective said, completing my sentence.

There was a knock at the open bedroom door.

"It's just the Professor and his wife in the house, guv," a uniformed constable reported.

"Knock up all the neighbours and check out their garages, their out houses and their gardens."

Some of this was new to me.

"Whatever this is, my wife has nothing to do with it," I protested mildly. Detective Inspector Danson did not seem to be the kind of cop who was going to be swayed – either way – by voluble pleas or expressions of innocence.

"What do you think this is?" The other man asked.

"If you'd asked me that twenty years ago I'd have been in a much better position to assist you in your inquiries, Inspector," I confessed ruefully. I shrugged, aware that the cuffs on my wrists were already feeling heavy. I was getting too old for this nonsense. "Nowadays, I keep my head down. What you see is pretty much what you get."

"Tell me about Abe?"

This was getting a little surreal.

Twenty minutes ago, I had been tucked up in bed with a woman half my age doing what dirty old men like me do in a situation like that; and now...

What was I doing?

Honestly and truly, I had no idea what was going on.

I was an eccentric has-been academic who owed his tenure at Long Island College, University of New York, to the fact that every old, respected, well-endowed faculty of higher learning traditionally had at least one or two oddballs among its Fellows. At LIC I was it, a sometime Professor of Colonial History, and the author of numerous hardly read books and dusty papers. Nobody was really interested in ancient history – my specialisation was the colonization of New England, and the formation of the thirteen original colonies – so these days I took a lot of classes and tutorials in mid-nineteenth century politics, supervised doctoral students and made peripatetic appearances at college functions in the role of court jester because nobody was remotely interested in the early days of settlement except Puritan fundamentalists and they did not tend to send their kids to notorious centres of Devil worship like the University of New York...

"Sorry," I realised Danson had asked me another question.

"Tell me about Abe, Professor?"

"He's a good kid."

"Have it your way," the policeman said. He shook his head and rose to his feet, beckoning me to follow him.

All the policeman, even the uniformed men were carrying firearms. It was about then that I started getting worried. In the German or Russian Empires every man in uniform carried a sword or a gun; throughout New Spain the Guardia Seville and the members of the various religious para-military orders routinely carried weapons but here, throughout New England – certainly east of the Mississippi and the Louisiana Country, most police officers recoiled in horror at the very notion of going about their duty with a six-shooter on their hip. Sure, out west most lawmen were armed but there was a reason they called places like the Oregon, North West and the Mountain Territories the 'Wild West'! Here in the 'first thirteen' colonies it was a matter of civic pride that some, at least, of the values of the old country were preserved, as if in aspic, in New England.

"Why all the guns, Inspector?" I asked as I was led outside to where a Bedford four-ton lorry and three Bentley police cars were parked. I could see there were other vehicles blocking each end of Clinton Road at the junction of Clinton and Jamaica Drive to the east and Flatbush Pike to the west.

Danson dropped onto the back seat of one of the cars beside me and patted the driver, a large, horsy woman in the dark blue uniform of the Long Island Constabulary.

"Straight back to the office, Mary."

"Where's the office?" I inquired, less than laconically. I was getting a tad panicky and made a concerted effort to get a grip.

"Hempstead, like I said," Danson replied. "Your wife will be taken to another station."

The detective was not New England born, there was an English West Country burr lingering deep down in his vowels that he had never made any attempt to cure.

"Sarah's done nothing..."

"Wrong? We shall see."

"Look," I tried again. "I don't know what this is about but if all this is," he reasoned, "is some kind of precautionary roundup because tomorrow is Empire Day..."

I heard my voice trail off into the ether.

Tomorrow was not exactly any old Empire Day.

1776 had been the year the American colonies had rebelled against the crown; and the decisive battle of that failed 'revolution' had been fought only a few miles from where they sat as the car bumped and rolled along the narrow Long Island roads towards Hempstead.

28th August would be the bicentennial of the crushing of the First American Rebellion...

While Hempstead was only some twenty miles from Gravesend as the crow flew until the work to widen the south coast pike was completed sometime next year it would take – even in the middle of the night with hardly any other traffic – over an hour to get to Hempstead. It was hardly any wonder that most non-religious Long Islanders were more worried about traffic jams and the abysmal state of the roads than they were about politics!

The last two winters had been long and hard, ice had got into men's bones like it had into fissures in the tarmac, neither the road crews or the island's hospitals had been able to cope with the harshness of the seasons. That was the trouble; when the Governor was a good man everything went well, ticketyboo, in fact, but when he was a dolt like the current incumbent the whole shebang soon went to Hell!

Not that all the ills of King's County, or any of the other three counties of Long Island were all the fault of the current Governor or of his office in Albany. The Colonial, County and District Councils all had to take their share of the blame; although, as friends and correspondents back in the old country were always telling him, the two Houses of Parliament, and the county and district system of national, supra-national and local governance 'at home' was hardly infallible. Of course, nobody in the British Isles had to suffer the additional executive-bureaucratic burden of having an imperial consul – the Viceroy, officially the Governor of the Commonwealth of New England – lording it over them from his palace in Philadelphia in between the Crown and the apparatus, or rather, the fig leaves of democracy. Whichever way one cut it no citizen of New England's vote counted in the way a man or a woman's vote did back in the so-called United Kingdom…

"So, what's your story, Inspector Danson?" I asked, curious to discover if the man was going to give me the silent treatment all the way to Hempstead. He had not risen to my baited remark about Empire Day.

"I came over here so long ago you could still get free passage if it was to take up a civil service appointment across the pond," the policeman answered, suppressing a wry chuckle. "Clerking didn't have much charm, or square-bashing with the militia so I went to night school, got a degree and joined the Colonial Police Service. That was in forty-nine. I moved down here from Boston five or six years ago. My wife's people come from Philadelphia."

"Do you have kids?"

"Two girls at college in New York. Garden City College."

"Oh right…"

"That was part of the deal when I transferred to Special Branch in the twin-colony," Danson freely admitted.

During the course of their shared histories New York and Long Island had parted company more than once. Eventually, the Colonial Office back in London had got fed up with the 'coming and going' and put its foot down. That had been back in 1902; but history never really goes away so even though most of those who were alive at the time were long dead and gone everybody in the Crown Colony of New York still referred to it as the 'twin-colony'.

"Do you and your sons ever talk about the 'old days', Professor?"

The question blind-sided me for a moment.

"I, yeah, well, you know...'

"This isn't part of the official police interview," Danson assured me. "We'll do all that later. When the tapes are running. I'm just interested. That's my problem. That's why I do what I do. I just like to know, to find out stuff, things."

"Yeah, I suppose I talked to the kids about why their old man was always getting locked up. Rachel always stepped in when I started proselytising. She was Lutheran, straight up and down and me, well I'm a confirmed agnostic about most things. None of the kids were ever interested in politics. I'd tell them history as stories, I reckon they thought I was telling them fairy tales when they were little and when they grew up they weren't interested. Isn't that always the way?"

"I reckon so. Why did Abe go up to Albany; there's a teaching hospital, St Paul's, in Manhattan?"

"He planned to specialise in research once he qualified. Churchill College has a really good post-grad regime."

I moved on quickly; the notion that Abe had planned all along to go into medical research was a fiction; albeit a useful fiction because it deferred both his colonial indenture to serve with the twin-colony public health service for not less than five years and kept his name off the draft lists for at least the next two, plus those indentured five years. Both Abe's brothers had jumped at the chance to go into the military; Abe was not like his brothers and when he had qualified for medical school Rachel had made damned sure her baby boy had got all his ducks in line.

"Besides, Abe likes it up there. We used to take family

vacations up in the Mohawk Country. We made a lot of friends over the years," I thought about it, suspecting it was a mistake to go on talking. Oddly, I did not think I had anything to be guilty about; old-timers like me had been outflanked by the 'Devolution not Revolution' movement years ago. Heck, in the last Colony-wide Legislative Council elections I had campaigned for and voted for the Social Democratic and Liberal Party! "I sort of lost contact with a lot of people up there after Rachel died. Setting up house with Sarah put a lot of people's noses out of joint, I suppose."

"What about Abe?"

"Abe was closer to his Ma than he was to me. Don't get me wrong, we were, still are, so far as I know, *tight* but a kid's always closer to his Ma or his Pa and Abe was always Rachel's 'little boy'."

"How did he feel about Sarah?"

"He missed his Ma; how do you think he felt about another woman coming into the family home?"

"Sorry, dumb question."

I did not get the impression Detective Inspector Danson asked a lot of 'dumb' questions. Not unless he had a good reason.

Chapter 2

HMS Lion, Upper Bay, New York

His Majesty George the Fifth, by the Grace of God of the United Kingdom of Great Britain and Northern Ireland and of His Other Realms and Territories King, Head of the Commonwealth, and Defender of the Faith was an early riser. Especially, when he was at sea with *his* Navy.

The Royal Marines attired in their dress redcoats – a hangover from another age which always rather jarred the King's sense of...perspective and seemed more and more out of place in this modern age - snapped to attention as he moved through the Royal suite of cabins in the battleship's aft superstructure on his way up to the quarterdeck for his morning constitutional and the one cigarette his beloved wife permitted him before breakfast without censure.

Because she thought smoking was bad for him.

Bless her...

His wife, Her Royal Highness Princess Eleanor, the Duchess of Windsor – because the hidebound fools his father had gathered around himself during his fifty-seven-year reign were petty-minded stick in the muds who had not believed she was of sufficiently 'high birth' to ever be deemed 'Queen' – was a late-riser, a minor incompatibility they had 'worked around' in their long and happy marriage. In any event, when they travelled together on Royal tours and suchlike they slept in separate quarters, and often, Eleanor was fully engaged on her own work connected to the many charities and educational foundations of which she was a patron, while he had to deal with the local 'politicos' and their ghastly 'mercantile' paymasters.

No, that was unfair...

In comparison with other colonial regimes he honestly believed that the British model was fundamentally, if not squeakily clean and proper, then infinitely less venal and corrupt than most of the other – foreign – ones he had encountered down the years.

The happiest days of his life had been the twenty-three years he had spent in the Royal Navy. While his three elder brothers had led unfulfilled wastrel lives readying themselves to assume, sooner or later or never at all, the full weight of the crown he, as the youngest, practically forgotten issue – his parents had been in their early forties at the time of his birth – of the house of Hanover-Gotha-Stewart, he had quietly graduated from the Britannia Royal Naval College at Dartmouth in 1941, been regarded with so little unction within the family that he had been permitted to marry a woman of middling aristocratic lineage whom he actually liked, to raise a family more or less out of the public eye and to pursue what in the end was a brilliant career cut short by the combined predations of age, alcohol, accidents and eventually, the murderous activities of the Irish Republican Army on Empire Day in 1962 upon the rest of his blood line.

His father, the late King had passed away in May 1962 and preparations had been well in hand for the Coronation of his surviving brother Edward until those blasted Fenians had intervened. He still missed 'Teddy', with who he had always enjoyed relatively cordial relations.

'You're a lucky beggar, Bertie!' Teddy had said to him wistfully a fortnight before his death. 'You've got Eleanor, the Navy, those well-adjusted, sensible boys and girls. All I'm going to end up with is the bloody Crown, which will set off my lumbago every time I put the damned thing on, a wife who can't stand the sight of me and two brattish sons who can't wait for me to shuffle off this mortal coil!'

Her Royal Highness Princess Sophia, Duchess of Cornwall, Albert the Duke of Northumberland and his brother Charles Duke of York had perished with Teddy, still at that time the titular Prince of Wales and Monarch uncrowned in Dublin fourteen years ago. Since both of Teddy's sons had died in the 1950s without male issue the 'family firm' had passed to George.

He had been well and truly 'lumbered' with it ever since!

By then he had attained the rank of Post Captain and was in command of the very ship upon whose quarterdeck he now strolled enjoying his morning cigarette.

HMS Lion had been half-way through her second commission in those days, less than four years old and in passage home from a world cruise in company with the old battlecruiser Vanguard and half-a-dozen fleet destroyers.

The Vanguard had gone to the breakers yard in the mid-sixties; a sad fate for the ship which had been the flagship of the greatest navy in the history of the World for over thirty years. There had been some discussion about dry docking her in perpetuity at Portsmouth but in the end the cost of maintaining such a leviathan as a mere 'museum ship' had decided her fate.

The King's old uniforms still fitted him, although a little snugly of late. His father and brothers had fleshed out from high living in middle age, in the process becoming the subject of numerous bucolic cartoons and endless ribaldry among the peoples of the Empire. That was the trouble with his family; it had grown fat on the prerogatives and privileges of the Monarchy and it was hardly surprising that at the time of his accession the whole institution was threatening to become an impotent fig leaf for the largesse and the indolence of the political classes in the second half of the twentieth century.

It had taken over ten minutes to proclaim *his* full titles upon his Coronation in Westminster Abbey. His father had still styled himself 'Emperor of India'!

Imperatoris India...

He had put a stop to that nonsense the day after the Coronation!

George V, Dei Gratia Britanniarum Regnorumque Suorum Ceterorum Rex, Consortionis Populorum Princeps, Fidei Defensor was more than a mouthful as it was!

Unfortunately, he could do little about actually still being King Emperor even though the political classes had been talking about Indian independence for decades.

He was still quite proud about the *Consortionis Populorum Princeps* honorific; pretending that the Crown Dominions of Canada, Australia and New Zealand were, in effect, imperial fiefdoms governed wholly from London had been a gratuitous misrepresentation of the true state of affairs for over fifty years.

If only some similar enlightened state of affairs existed in New England!

Not that there was the remotest prospect that the twenty-nine fiercely independent, constantly disputatious crown colonies, dependent territories, protectorates and provinces of the North American continent filling the vast hinterland from coast to coast, and north to south between Canada and the lands of the Empire of New Spain, were ever going to unite, or form any kind of union, commonwealth let alone nation in his, or he suspected, sadly, in his lifetime or that of his children or grandchildren.

Perversely, in fact, it was the very 'independence' – particularly of the First Thirteen colonies, each from each other – which ensured the continuing allegiance of *all* the other North American territories. Nobody wanted to be ruled by 'those bloody Virginians', or Bostonians, or by those Connecticut and Rhode Island puritans, or by those planters in the Carolinas, or by the conniving merchants and bankers in New York, et al. And as for all those industrialists in Pennsylvania, the Ohio Territory and the former Indian country provinces south of the Great Lakes – Indiana, Ohio, Illinois, Michigan and the South Algonquin Territory – well, what business did people like that have dictating to the East

Coast? Nobody imagined that the vast tracts of the once French Illinois-Louisiana lands, the roadless counties and shires of the great prairies at the heart of the continent, still separated, fragmented by the hunting grounds of the ancient tribes despite the railways now connecting the Oregon and Vancouver territories to the Dakotas, and thence to the rest of the continent, wanted any part of any kind of union with the 'English' colonies in the east; they had far more in common with their Canadian neighbours. It was only the south western border outlying territories and proto-colonies, particularly those whose boundaries abutted with the unmarked, barely mapped and forever contested limits of Spanish Alta California, Nuevo Mexico, Coahuila and West Texas, which had never stopped demanding 'strength in unity'.

Soon after his accession, his ministers had tried to persuade the King to marry off his youngest daughter, Caroline, to the heir to the Spanish thrown. He had put his foot down; there would be no more 'royal weddings' of that kind. Little good had such 'arranged' matches done his family; all that conniving and Machiavellian manoeuvring back in the eighteenth and nineteenth century had resulted in the war to end all wars a little over a hundred years ago!

The King flicked his cigarette butt over the side of the ship.

Lion had led her three fifty thousand-ton sisters through the narrows – Hell's Gate in olden times - into the Upper Bay at dawn and now the 5th Battle Squadron was anchored in line ahead in the main channel with Bucking Island and Bedford Island to port and Governor's Island to the starboard, with the bows of the four castles of steel pointing straight up the Hudson River.

As the early morning haze cleared the King gazed thoughtfully at HMS Princess Royal, and behind her the Queen Elizabeth – ships named respectively for his elder sister Margaret Rose and for his mother – and the Tiger, returning for the first time to the waters into which she had been launched over two decades ago.

To the east, hidden by the urban and industrial sprawl at least two great new vessels were under construction in the Brooklyn Admiralty Dockyard at Wallabout Bay; but not armour-encased fast battleships like the 'Big Cats' and her sisters of the Lion class. No, the future lay, it seemed in the air now that all the great powers had agreed to scrap their undersea fleets.

Or rather, to build no more of the infernal craft!

The King loathed politics.

The 'Submarine Treaty' crisis had almost caused a general world war just two years into his reign. The Germans and their fair-weather allies, Japan, feeling that their 'imperial rights' had been frustrated for too long had never really wanted to go to war with the British Empire but when the Russians had decided – for reasons nobody could explain – to use the age-old chaos in China to seize a 'buffer zone' in Manchuria and blundered into a confrontation with the Japanese the British Government – *His* Government – had started issuing ultimatums right left and centre!

Nonetheless, as *His* Prime Minister – he had had six thus far in his reign - had complacently assured him back in 1965, 'every cloud has a silver lining'.

International diplomacy was about understanding what the other fellow actually wanted. Invariably, to get to the nub of the matter one had to discard practically everything everybody actually said!

The Germans wanted the international status of their 'possessions' and 'concessions' in Africa 'clarified', specifically their right to hold and administer the mostly desert province of South West Africa and one or two territories on the shore of the Indian Ocean, while the Japanese wanted to be left to get on with whatever they were up to in China. Luckily for all concerned by then the Russians just wanted the war with the Japanese to stop.

In any event, the King had travelled to Berlin and Moscow and behind the scenes finessed the bare bones of a quid pro quo in which the British Empire underwrote 'adjustments to the colonial governance of regions in southern Africa' and in league with the Germans quietly mediated a cessation of hostilities in the Far East; and with a collective sigh of relief the British Empire had not got into a ruinously expensive new undersea arms race.

Even though he was the captain of a battleship at the time the King had been utterly unaware of the momentous, literally earth-shaking scientific advances preoccupying his ministers and his superiors at the Admiralty back in 1962.

Of course, within a year of his accession the genie had been well and truly out of the bottle but at the time he had been utterly flabbergasted to learn that Pandora's Box was about to be flung open!

The atomic age had been about to dawn.

City destroying bombs the size of a small dinghy!

Limitless peaceful power supplies!

Submarines the size of battleships which could steam around the globe underwater ten times without needing to refuel...

The idea of having one's cities demolished by a single aircraft carrying a single bomb was bad enough; the idea of submarines so formidable that all existing surface navies would become obsolete in less than a generation had horrified the Admiralty, and axiomatically, the King's ministers. It was one thing to get involved in an arm's race one could win; another entirely, getting into one everybody understood nobody could ever win.

Thus, nuclear power would stay, for the moment above the waves signifying that the future lay in the air which in turn had spurred every major power to deluge previously unimagined, impossibly large quantities of treasure upon their new aerospace industries. The first fruits of all this investment in research and development had been the revolutionary 'jet' aircraft now undergoing testing in the British and German Empires.

Virtually overnight aircraft carriers, until then the poor relations of the battlefleet equipped with flimsy, short-range and low performance first and second-generation propeller driven scouts and fighters, had never needed to be over-large. However, in the coming age in which it was anticipated that heavyweight jet-powered aircraft ten times the weight and operating with landing and take-off speeds perhaps five to six times faster than their lightweight forebears would have to be accommodated, it was clear that the new breed of fleet carrier were going to have to be huge beasts.

Both the ships under construction in the monstrous Wallabout Bay dry docks were forty-thousand-ton behemoths with flight decks nearly a thousand feet long. They were to be equipped with great steam catapults capable of flinging twenty-ton aircraft into the air and of steaming at up to thirty-three knots. At yards around the Empire – at Halifax in Nova Scotia, Rosyth in Scotland, Birkenhead on the River Mersey and East London on the Thames, and at Norfolk in Virginia – other King George V class ships were on the slips.

'Why the Devil didn't I know anything about this atomic business?' The King had demanded that momentous day in July 1962.

'It was not felt that you needed to know, Your Majesty,' he had been informed.

The Empire's 'bomb project' – code-named 'Blue Danube' – had been, and still was mainly based in New England, albeit a long way away from the curious eyes of most colonists in Tennessee, the badlands of the Dakotas and the mountains and forests of British Columbia. Other than that the Empire had its own 'bomb' – tested in 1966 off Christmas Island, and subsequently at the Montebello Islands, off the Pilbara coast of Western Australia in 1967 and 1968 – the man in the street throughout the Empire was blissfully unaware of the true history of the Anglo-German and now Anglo-German-Russian nuclear bomb race.

Thank God...

"Good morning, sir."

The respectful salutation broke the King out of his brooding introspection. He turned to face Rear Admiral Sir Thomas Packenham, Flag Officer Commanding 5th Battle Squadron.

Like his monarch Packenham was wearing his Blue No. 3 – general duties - dress uniform. There would be plenty of time later to don their full No. 1 ceremonial 'rags'. For the moment they were comfortable in their double-breasted reefer jackets over white long-sleeved shirts and blue ties. Although the King was entitled to wear a rig which boasted enough gold braid to sink a medium-sized barge on his jacket sleeves – he was after all, among other things, Admiral of the Fleet – he never wore more than the four rings he had earned in his years of professional service when he was onboard a Royal Navy ship.

"I gather the weather is set fair, Tom?" The Squadron Commander had been at Dartmouth with the King and the two men and their families had been very close ever since. Time and again in recent years William Hugh George Albert Hanover-Gotha-Stewart – he had always been called 'Bertie' in the family and by his wide circle of friends in the Navy – had been thankful for those long years of grace when he had lived as a relatively normal man, and for the large number of 'real' lifelong friends he had made in that interregnum. One such was Tom Packenham.

"Yes, sir." The two men gazed at the other 'Lions' moored

astern of the flagship like immovable castles of steel rising out of the cold waters of the bay.

The battleships and their escorts were streaming huge Union Jacks at their bow and stern jack staffs, and White Ensigns and battle flags carrying the names of the actions in which they, and their namesakes had fought in since the birth of the Royal Navy from their towering steel fore and aft masts. For all that there had been no *great war* since the 1860s there had hardly been a year during the last century when the Royal Navy had not seen battle.

In a funny way the shock of the atomic age had initially pacified many previously dangerous hot spots around the globe; temporarily quashing the persistent local, often very nasty, colonial spats and uprisings which were the bane of the all mature Empires. Lately, trouble seemed to spark where one least expected it; one year prompted by the threat of famine in Bengal, the separatist movements in South East Asia, tribal conflict in Arabia, this or that clan feuding with its neighbours in sub-Saharan Africa, piracy in the Mediterranean or the Caribbean, or the latest unrest along the desert and mountain wilderness border between New England-Nuevo Spain. People too easily forgot that it was less than twenty years since a rebellion against the Spanish authorities in Florida had drawn in sympathetic militias from the neighbouring colonies of the Carolinas and Georgia, during which the Mississippi Counties of Louisiana had sent raiders into Texas – Tejas, the eastern department of the State of Coahuila – in a clumsy land-grab that had almost embroiled the rump of European Spain in a Mediterranean war and caused a North Atlantic stand-off between the antiquated Spanish Fleet and the Royal Navy off Cape Trafalgar. Things had escalated so far out of hand that at one juncture Spanish troops threatened to assault Gibraltar!

The idea that the Spanish would contemplate pitting a rag-tag collection of obsolete ironclads against the might of the battle line of the Mediterranean Fleet was frankly absurd; nevertheless, the Government of the day in England had fallen over that particular debacle.

These days, the trouble was that one never knew where the next problem was coming from! As the first of the King's Prime Ministers had remarked when asked what worried him the most: 'Events. Events, sir!'

"My father always used to say that it made him nervous when the sun shone on Empire Day," the King guffawed softly. "That was why he hated to go abroad in July."

His old friend echoed his mood.

"What is it they say? The two things you can rely on in England are that it will rain but never enough to stop Australia or the Philadelphians beating England at cricket!"

The two men had switched their gaze to the old-fashioned ironclad moored in the grey waters between Governor's Island and Red Hook. The twenty thousand ton white-hulled battleship belonged to a generation twice removed from that of the Lion and her mighty sisters.

The *Nuestra Señora de la Santísima Trinidad* had been the pride of the Armada de Nuevo Española when she was launched in 1927; that she was nominally still the flagship of the Gulf of Spain Fleet was in part a testament to the decline of the once formidable Spanish Navy, and also a minor but presumably calculated slight to her English hosts. The Spanish had sent the old ship – she had been dry docked in Havana for over ten years acting as the non-operational flagship, essentially the shore-based headquarters of the small but otherwise relatively modern Cuban Squadron - up to New York simply to make a statement about how little importance the administration in Madrid attached to the day.

"They say they removed the breech blocks of her big guns and de-activated the hydraulic trains for both turrets," the King said, thinking out aloud.

The calibre of the guns of the old battleship's main armament was the same as that of the four Lions' and all thirty-one of the big-gun capital ships on the current Navy list; but HMS Lion's guns were 15-inch 42-calibre Mark V versions of a naval rifle found to be so reliable and accurate that it had been the standard heavy gun of the Royal Navy for over five decades. Its characteristics – including how to adjust gunnery tables to compensate for barrel lining degradation during its 150 to 180-round service life – were intimately understood, and over the years it had been established that its design maximum range of approximately 33,500 yards could be safely extended, by supercharging with additional propellant well within the bursting tolerance of the barrel, to 37,800 yards. Moreover, although the Royal Navy had always prided itself on its ability to put the greatest possible weight of metal in the air at any one time in a battle, by tradition and pragmatic trial and error it had been proven beyond reasonable doubt that the optimum 'accurate' rate of controlled fire of the Mark V was approximately – give or take three or four seconds - two rounds per minute. Theoretically, five rounds every two minutes could be fired, but this always tended to reduce the effectiveness of the 'shooting'.

The *Santísima Trinidad's* four big guns were 38-calibre like her secondary armament of eight single casemate-mounted 9.5-inch weapons. Unlike the naval rifles carried by Royal Navy ships the Spanish ironclad's guns were the originals, 'shot out' as long ago as the 1940s, and even in their prime had had only two-thirds of the range of the British Mark Vs. In her long ago prime the old Spanish ironclad had only been able to make sixteen or seventeen knots. Back during Lion's second commission she had clocked thirty-two and a half knots – nearly thirty-seven miles an hour – running machinery trials off the west coast of Scotland and sustained a speed of thirty point two knots during a two-hour maximum power run.

"The Spaniard's escorts look well turned out," the King observed, enjoying this last moment of the day when he could get away with just being an old sea dog.

The latest class of Spanish destroyers – less gunships and more general-purpose frigates with a couple of guns forward and twin anti-aircraft missile rails aft – were German-built and looked a little top-heavy with their ELDAR masts and boxy, aluminium-skinned superstructures.

"One good hit and they're done for," retorted the Commander of the 5th Battle Squadron.

"Maybe," the King replied. For the moment the forest of smaller calibre automatic-firing anti-aircraft barrels carried by most large Royal Navy ships probably remained the best option for fending off air attack. But in five years' time when the first of the new jet fighters and bombers came on the scene, perhaps precision guided missilery would be the only thing that could be relied upon to do the job.

The Navy certainly thought that was the way the wind was blowing. The next time Lion or her sisters went into dock for a major overhaul all their quadruple 1.7-inch mounts were going to be removed, new ELDARS hoisted and short-range – two to four miles – surface-to-air – missile launchers installed amidships on either side of the aft funnel.

The King was aware that, as was their wont, the men of his protection detail had moved closer as he had been taking the air on the 'exposed' quarterdeck of the battleship. The nearby islands were swarming with colonial policemen and soldiers from the New York Garrison. The next nearest shore was well over a mile away; if some misguided fool wanted to take a pot shot at him from that sort of range through the morning haze good luck to him!

Oddly, it was at the very moment that this thought flitted across his mind that he heard a dull 'clunk' somewhere to his left. He might have heard another 'pinging' sound a second or so later but by then he was buried beneath a wall of muscular bodies, everybody was shouting and the thunder of booted feet on the planking of the quarter deck was deafening.

Strong hands picked him up and transported him as if he was weightless towards, around and behind the barbette of 'Y' main battery turret. Then, after the briefest of hesitation he was bundled unceremoniously down an ammunition loading hatchway into the heavily armoured innards of the giant floating citadel.

Chapter 3

I had been arrested under a warrant that permitted the Long Island Police to hold me in custody for seventy-two hours subsequent to the moment of my detention. Basically, I was going nowhere for the next few days.

The ordinary uniformed 'bobbies' at East Hempstead were unnervingly like their fathers, two or three decades ago when I had been a frequent caller and guest at establishments such as the brand new whitewashed, spic and span station on the Jamaica Bay Road just out of town, in former times and were, in the main, regular guys. Of course, years ago, there were no women in the police force, that was an eye-opener, being processed into custody by a female sergeant. She was hardly Sarah's age, brunette, pregnant and not in the mood to be messed about by a shaggy-haired disgraced professor feebly trying to make light of his situation.

I tried to sleep but my neck was sore from being rousted out of bed and manhandled to the floor in the middle of the night. Oh, and I was worried about Abe. I had been worried about my youngest son since he was knee high, truth be known. Rachel had been too protective, too...nurturing; although that might just have been me being pig-headed.

When Inspector Danson had asked me about why Abe had chosen to study at Albany I had skated around the truth in more than one respect. Much though Abe and the other kids had loved those weeks we spent camping in the woods along the Mohawk River every year; I was a little afraid the sins of the father were about to be revisited on my family and suddenly I was thinking again of my old friend Tsiokwaris – in Kanien'kehára, the language of the Mohawk nation, 'Black Raven', and his daughter Tekonwenaharake, 'her voice travels through the wind'.

Rachel had wanted the kids to be exposed to the ways and the traditions of the indigenous native peoples of the colony; I had wanted to plumb the natural well of dissent and possibly, revolution in the ranks of the People of the Flint – the Mohawks - and their brother nations for once upon a time, long ago, I had not been the pacifistic, armchair rebel of my later years.

Rachel and the kids had burned a lot of that revolutionary zeal out of me early on. After that I was a dabbler, a dilettante dissident and little more. At first, I saw the peoples of the Iroquois 'league', as the French called them, as the separatist movement's natural allies. The Iroquois or Haudenosaunee – made up of the six tribes of the Cayuga, Mohawk, Onondaga, Oneida, Seneca, and Tuscarora peoples had survived the rapacity of the first waves of nineteenth century Anglo-European colonization and retained their identity, their sense of being a people.

I think my old friend Tsiokwaris thought I was a harmless, amusing fool. He was wise and patient, I was anything but; the fact of the matter was that to the tribes of the Iroquois Nation the colonies' ongoing respect for the sanctity of the tribal lands – south of Lake Eerie and Ontario and the St Lawrence, mirrored by the Dominion of Canada to the north – which had finally ended the Indian Wars in the late eighteenth century, meant that there had never been any real appetite in the Mohawk, or any of the other Iroquois peoples to wage war again on the white men. Other that is than when periodically, one or other of the cronies of colonial administration bigwigs in Albany attempted to grant logging or mining concessions adjacent to or infringing upon their 'countries'.

As far back as the late eighteenth century the English had figured out that it was easier to live in peace with the

Iroquois and the Algonquin and most of the other Indian nations than it was to get embroiled in a continental-scale never-ending guerrilla war which would sooner or later, bankrupt the colonies and the old country.

Tsiokwaris and his people understood that calculus and counter-intuitively, the drive to pen the native peoples back into their ancestral lands which had slowly gathered pace over the last thirty or forty years had suited the Mohawk just fine.

In retrospect Rachel and I brought our little family into contact with that other, indigenous New England of the native tribes at the very cusp of a sea change in the affairs of the First Thirteen colonies; that moment when co-existence, the byword – something of an article of faith - of generations of settlers for over a hundred years which had kept the continental peace was falling out of fashion.

In any event, I had come to understand that the Iroquois had a different, more elastic, spiritual connection to the land than was fathomable to most white men and women; and had no need to be lectured by a 'settler' – for that was what all white and black men in New England were to most native Americans of the North East – about the legacy of invasion and oppression.

I was an idiot back in those days!

In my defence I was an idealistic idiot; not that that is any real defence as anybody who has tried to rely on it in a court of law will attest.

The real reason Abe had applied to Churchill College, Albany, was Tekonwenaharake, 'Kate'. She and Abe were of an age and the two of them had been peas out of the same pod from the day they first rubbed noses when they were three years old.

Tekonwenaharake translated as *her voice travels through the wind* in English but her father stoically maintained that it sounded even more poetic in the native Kanien'kehában.

Kate had grown up a full head short of Abe, the tallest of the three brothers at six feet and a fraction of an inch, and her slim litheness was like poetry in motion compared to Abe's gangling clumsiness as a teenager. Abe had thickened out a bit, turned into the family's one, real sportsman in his last couple of years at Grammar School. He had been too whole-hearted playing football, a little prone to get himself injured chasing lost causes; at cricket he had been a star with bat or ball, and his big hands never dropped a catch. All things considered, Abe had been exactly the 'late developer' his mother had said he always would be.

And as soon as he could he had run away to Albany to be with Kate. Sarah and I had fretted about that. He had a brilliant career ahead of him; Kate might be a girl in a million but...

She was pure bred Mohawk and in the professions; in any profession, everybody knew that if he married her Abe could kiss his career goodbye.

Rachel had said 'Abe's happiness is the only thing that matters'.

After she died I lost my bearings; my moral compass went awry and like a fool I had had 'that conversation' with Abe. It had not gone very well.

'It's none of my business,' I had confessed.

He had confirmed that he was of the same mind.

I had rowed back.

'You know I'll support you whatever you decide...'

Abe had come home a lot less after that.

Kate was the one non-negotiable thing in my youngest son's life and now I was asking myself if that was what all this was about.

For all I knew Abe had married the girl by now; that was a thing easily achieved in the Mohawk country, a simple matter of words exchanged between the prospective husband of a young woman and her father or guardian elder.

In theory Kate's views would not actually have been canvassed but in practice, having known the kid since she was knee high, it would have been the *only* thing my old friend Tsiokwaris would have taken into account.

Heck, why did life have to be so goddamned complicated?

At around ten o'clock I was escorted into a small, well-ventilated windowless interview room on the first floor of the police station.

A blond woman in her twenties brought in mugs of tea and joined Detective Inspector Danson on the opposite side of the room's single table. She had entered the room juggling the mugs on a tin tray with a slim brown attaché case under her left arm.

Danson had relieved her of the tray so she could divest herself of her case, which she dropped on one of the chairs, and wordlessly delved inside. I registered the small black notebook and the silvery propelling pencil, or pen, which she withdrew from it before putting it on the floor by the nearest table leg.

I tried to wake up.

I had been brought a cooked breakfast from the station canteen, allowed to wash and perform my personal ablutions in private in a washroom at the end of the corridor nearest my holding cell, and nobody had bothered to re-cuff me after I had been processed into custody in the small hours.

I sipped my tea.

There was a waist high-to-ceiling mirror across the end wall of the interview room; presumably a two-way mirror to permit the full observation of proceedings. From past experience I automatically assumed that there would be microphones buried in the walls, too.

Interview rooms had been dirty, smelly places in the old days. It appeared that things had moved on more than somewhat since the last time I had been in police custody.

Another pleasant surprise was that the tea was only

middlingly vile.

"Sorry," the young woman apologised. She sounded very English. Her blond hair was cut short, almost like a man's and her freckles took years off her age.

Danson stirred.

"This is Lieutenant Judith Adams of the Royal Military Police," he announced. "She is a member of His Majesty's Personal Security Detail and for the duration of the Royal Visit to New York, New Jersey and Long Island she is acting as the Redcaps' Liaison Officer with the Special Branch of the Colonial Police Service."

"Delighted to meet you, Lieutenant," I muttered.

What the fuck was going on?

Danson sat back, clearly leaving the floor to the woman.

"Inspector Danson tells me that you haven't seen or spoken to your son for several days, Professor Fielding?"

"Weeks, actually. Last time we spoke was about a month ago, I suppose..."

"Yes," the young woman said, checking something in the notebook she had opened. "That would have been on 8th June. You spoke for about five minutes." She hesitated, frowned. "About little of any substance. Our analysts could not rule out the possibility that you were communicating using a code employing keywords. Prior to that you spoke on 23rd May. This conversation was a little less stilted, likewise not obviously suspicious."

Lieutenant Adams looked up.

"Yes, we were tapping your phone line. We also tapped your office line at the Long Island College and you and your wife have been under surveillance for the last five weeks.'

She could have bowled me over with a very small feather!

"I don't..."

"Understand?" The woman queried abruptly. "No. Neither do we. That is a profoundly unsatisfactory state of affairs."

The woman had switched from a tray-bearing human being to a mountain lioness with her prey in her sights.

It was all I could do to stop myself apologising.

"I spoke to your wife earlier, Professor Fielding. Colleagues of mine will interrogate her again later this morning when," she sniffed, "she is a little less distraught."

I began to react.

Angrily.

I opened my mouth to object but was beaten to the punch.

"You and your wife," the woman snarled, "will be at liberty to protest about your treatment *when* the clear and present threat to His Majesty the King has been dealt with. Until that time please understand that any failure to fully co-operate with my inquiries will be referred to the appropriate prosecuting authorities under the auspices of the Treachery Act. Do I make myself clear, Professor Fielding?"

'Yes...'

Okay, now I am a professional historian so I know a little bit about how the British – in the colonies the generic term 'English' is interchangeable with 'British', although in fact the Empire was carved out by Scottish, Welsh and Irish folk in equal measure to the 'English' – had carved out and up until now, have managed against all the odds, to hang onto the biggest Empire in the annals of planet Earth.

Granted, New Spain controlled – well, sort of – huge tracts of land in the Americas, and of course, the Philippines. Portugal still nominally runs its Brazilian Empire and various other lumps of territory in Africa and Far East. One ought not to discount the German Empire, which oversees most of Central Europe and the Balkans as well as miscellaneous African territories. Then there were those beastly Ottomans based in the Turkish littoral and dominating the Middle East, not to mention the increasingly despotic Romanovs and their ramshackle disaster area excuse for an imperium of all the Russias, or the kingdom of the medieval, much preyed upon Chinese now half-occupied by the Japanese.

However, the British Empire was different; it was bigger than the next two biggest put together, richer than any three or four of the others, better and more efficiently run, and square mile for square mile, much cheaper to maintain and therefore intrinsically more sustainable. All the other 'empires' had to bankrupt themselves and impoverish, to one degree or another, sections of their own populations to finance the armies required to hold down their far-flung lands; not the British, they had the Navy and, in most places, they let the locals get on with the business of business relatively unmolested. The steel mills of New England alone out-produced the entire German Empire, the cotton mills of England clothed half the World, five ships of every six built was constructed in British or American yards, the prairies of Canada and the crown territories beyond the Great Lakes supplied half the globe's grain, Australasia a third of the meat on and off the hoof, a traveller could walk from Alexandria to the Cape of Good Hope without once stepping off British soil, and the oilfields of Persia and the East Indies kept the greatest navy ever to steam the seas under way.

But none of these things were the real keys to the greatness of the British Empire. The reason it had come out of the chasing pack and attained a position of such apparently impregnable dominance was very simple.

When push came to shove the British – well, mostly the English – were utterly ruthless.

If a thing needed to be done; it was done!

That was why nobody had been so stupid as to pick a stand-up fight with the British for over a hundred years; and the Pax Britannica was, to all intents, complete.

Wags in London Clubs and throughout that part of the global atlas painted forever Imperial pink, men winked and nudged each other and boasted that the only place the English had ever 'given up on' was Afghanistan; and that was only to give the Romanovs an itch that they could never scratch, let alone eradicate!

Just like the Emperor Hadrian back in the early years of the second century had decided that the Roman Empire was big enough as it was, the British had called time on the 'era of expansion' to secure the peace of Paris' in 1865, and the World Order which had emerged from that congress had, more or less, guaranteed the peace ever since.

The so-called Imperial 'compromise' had only been so successful because all the other powers understood that whoever stepped out of line first would discover that...the British were absolutely ruthless!

Such was the perfectly constructed geopolitical strategic calculus which had governed the affairs of the World for over a century.

Lieutenant Adams's closed her black notebook and fixed me with her blue-grey eyes.

"We will address the question of your loyalty to the Crown at another time, Professor. Right now, what is going to happen is that you are going to give me every possible assistance in my inquiries. Do we understand each other?"

My throat was dry, constricted.

For a moment I was afraid I was going to have a panic attack. I glanced involuntarily towards the mirrored wall to my right.

Who was listening?

"Do we understand each other?" The woman repeated, sensing my momentary mental disintegration.

I nodded.

"Yes..."

Chapter 4

HMS Lion, Upper Bay, New York

Eleanor, Duchess of Windsor, could not – try as she might – stop herself fussing around her husband. She had been fast asleep when the shots had been fired at the King and not known what all the excitement was about when the great ship had burst into life all around her. She had heard the news first from one of her junior ladies in waiting.

Lady Jane Dreyer-Mayne was the middle daughter of one of her friends at St Johns College where she had spent three blissful years after escaping Cheltenham Ladies College in 1938. Going up to Oxford had delayed the awful day her parents – dear people but *so old fashioned about these things* – attempted to marry her off to some hopeless dunce of 'a similar or slightly elevated social standing', so they were not saddled with her upkeep for the rest of her days.

But that was another story; that morning her lady in waiting, who was a new addition to the royal retinue and still feeling her feet in the role – basically, as her mistress's appointment secretary, odd-job girl and her genteel gatekeeper – was flushed and very jumpy.

"His Majesty was walking and somebody fired at him from the Long Island side of the bay..."

Eleanor had not really been awake.

"What..."

"The King is all right! Oh, sorry, I should have said that first, I..."

The older woman had ended up having to comfort the frightened girl. Eleanor quickly discovered that her husband's only injury was a knock to the brow incurred in the excitement as his bodyguards carried him out of harm's way; and that he was presently being attended to by the battleship's surgeon.

The telephone in her cabin rang. Lady Jane picked up. Apparently, HMS Lion's Captain wanted to speak to her and put her mind at rest.

"Thank you, that will not be necessary. I shall dress and go to my husband in due course."

No sooner had she put the phone down than Lady Jane blurted out that 'one of the bodyguards was wounded!'

Although, mercifully, not seriously.

A bullet had grazed his right hip.

'We,' Bertie always insisted, 'must be calm while all around us lose their heads, Ellie. That is our job. That is why we are the ones who live in the great palaces and are feted and acclaimed, and inevitably, sometimes abused, wherever we go.'

'Rather like the boy left standing on the burning deck,' she would observe and they would smile, one to the other because in this as in so many things they were of one mind.

Graceful as a swan outside; paddling like a lost duckling inside.

Bertie had burned practically all his bridges marrying a virtual commoner such as she. She was a Spencer, once upon a time her family had infiltrated the dynastic lines of half of Europe; however, those days were history, mostly pre-1860s and her father had hardly had the wherewithal to keep the family's Northamptonshire pile at Althorp standing by the time she met her future husband.

Bertie had just refused a posting to the Royal Yacht at the time so he was in particularly bad odour with his father, who had been dead set on bringing him back into the regal fold. The upshot had been that Bertie found himself posted to the Hong Kong station for the next two years.

To Eleanor their first encounter had been a pleasant evening; and their subsequent dinner in London about a month later, equally 'fun'. Prince Albert had behaved with the utmost decorum, been charming, amusing and kissed her hand as they parted that evening.

She had thought that was that until his first letter arrived.

'Dear Miss Spencer,' goodness, how sweetly formal that sounds now, 'As I mentioned during our recent most convivial meetings it is my fate to be exiled to the East for a spell. Might I impose on you so as to make my time away more bearable?'

They must have written each other two or three hundred letters over the course of the next twenty-six months. For her part she had refused to discuss or to disclose the substance of her correspondence to her father or mother, and especially not her sisters, all of whom were the most terrible gossips. During that period, she had also turned down two proposals of marriage, including one from a prosperous Virginia planter twice her age visiting England looking for a wife, his first having perished without issue of some local malady. Eleanor's mother had put the man up to it.

Bertie had proposed to her the day after he arrived back in England and the rest was, well, history...

This had provoked a dreadful schism within the Royal Family.

The old King was so upset he had refused to issue letters patent therefore before Bertie's accession to the throne she had never been 'Your Royal Highness', or really a 'Princess' of any kind in exactly the same way she was not, strictly speaking, actually the 'Queen' even now. Other, that was than in the hearts of many of her husband's subjects.

Bertie had never been a big one for all that nonsense; just because the bloody Arch Bishop of Canterbury and the Prime Minister of the day had a problem with crowning her Queen upon his Coronation he had made it known on the day of his accession that anybody who failed to address 'my wife as anything other than *Your Majesty* will be in trouble!'

In the end the Church, Parliament and the Prime Minister had suggested that officially she be styled Princess Eleanor, Duchess of Windsor thereafter.

Bertie, bless him, simply referred to her in public as 'the Queen'.

Honestly and truly, it was a mystery to her how the Empire had knocked along so well for so long; a mystery in exactly the same way it was no mystery at all why it was in so much trouble now.

Like her husband Eleanor blamed the old King, his courtiers and the nincompoops who had been running 'the circus' for much of the last century and whatever her reservations about the present administration in Whitehall, she and Bertie were of one mind where their duty lay. Somebody had to paper over the cracks while the Empire's crumbling foundations were if not repaired, then shored up for another generation or two!

"I don't understand why you were strutting about on the deck in full sight in the first place?" She whispered.

Her husband was sitting on a chair in the sick bay – more a fully-equipped floating hospital – in the bowels of the battleship. His recently stitched left eyebrow was still weeping and a nurse, one of the dozen or so onboard the flagship – periodically dabbed the decreasing dribble of blood.

Actually, Eleanor knew exactly why her husband had been walking the quarterdeck at such an ungodly hour of the morning. He was a creature of habit. He was the same at home. He walked the corridors of Buckingham Palace, or Sandringham, or Balmoral at or before the crack of dawn to compose himself for the coming day.

"They recovered a bullet from the deck just where you'd been walking, Bertie!"

Eleanor realised her husband had taken her right hand in his.

"Sorry, I'm making a scene," she apologised.

Her husband smiled wanly and glanced meaningfully around the compartment.

"We are surrounded by friends here," he murmured. And waved at the nearest bulkhead: "and by several inches of the best cemented armour plate that the master forgers of Sheffield can produce, my love."

Eleanor pulled herself together.

"So, what is our plan of action today?"

"We carry on as normal."

She accepted this without demur, leaned forward and kissed her husband's brow, well away from his wound.

"I shall make sure they put out the right uniform." She ran a hand over her hair. "I must look a mess, that will never do," she declared.

The King took his wife's hand anew.

"My dear, you are ever as beautiful to me as the day we wed."

"Men!" She whispered, sniffing back a tear as she made her departure.

Both Eleanor's sisters had had that high-cheeked, willowy natural 'look' that all the fashion magazines worshipped. She was shorter by an inch or so, less busty and a lot less preoccupied with what she looked like although that first night she had dined with Bertie, she had spent most of the previous afternoon in front of a mirror trying to get her face 'just right', never realising that he had probably already decided that she was perfect the way she was.

In retrospect, in exactly the same way she had decided he was...*the one*.

Albeit the unattainable, impossible *one*, whom a girl like her was never, ever going to live happily ever after.

Cinderella, you shall go to the ball...

All those years living as a detached member of the Royal

Family, politely and sometimes not so politely shunned by 'the family' now seemed so long ago as to belong to a lost age.

She had assumed that Bertie would speak fluent German, discovered that his father and his brothers apart, the rest of the family detested the language. Oh, he could speak it at a pinch, badly, you had to in the circles in which he had been raised but he was not fluent in German in the way he was in French or Spanish, the languages of the 'old enemies'.

Eleanor had taken German lessons to appease the old King; a waste of time. It must have been horribly galling for the surviving members of the Court to have to kow-tow to a brazen little hussy gold-digger from Northamptonshire when Bertie became King.

She and Bertie had promised each other that there would be no settling of old scores. Everybody started with a clean slate. Bertie planned to run a tight ship in which each and every member of the crew got a fair chance to show his or her mettle.

He was the accidental King; and she was his unlikely Guinnevere.

Eleanor was tempted to pinch herself some days.

It was as if she was living inside a fairy tale.

Tomorrow, Bertie and she would board a destroyer to review the fleet, or rather, fleets; half the Atlantic Fleet would be moored in the Lower Bay, there would be flypasts, visits to several big, and small ships of the visiting navies. As well as the Spanish the Portuguese, the Germans and the Japanese had sent impressive flotillas to New York.

The Germans had sent three battleships.

The Japanese had sent a couple of cruisers and several destroyers on a round the world cruise just so that they might be represented at the Empire Day celebrations.

However, today the Royal Party was due to visit the

Admiralty Dockyard at Wallabout Bay, there to launch the new anti-aircraft cruiser Polyphemus, and to partake of luncheon with the Governor of the twin state of New York-Long Island, before going across the East River to tour the city – which ought not to take too long because it only occupied the lower couple of miles of Manhattan Island – and to inspect various military bases and take the salute at a march past at Battery Field, the site of a fort in former times. That evening the Governor of New England would formally welcome the King to the Americas ahead of a banquet to be held in his honour in the ballroom of the biggest hotel in the city, the Savoy.

Tomorrow, Viscount De L'Isle, the Governor of New England, would join the Royal Party for the Empire Day Fleet Review, and the evening's state banquet at the mansion of the Lieutenant Governor of the Crown Colony of New Jersey in Elizabethtown.

Eleanor always approached days like this with a deliberately positive spirit but the day had hardly started and already some idiot had taken a pot shot at her husband!

Chapter 5

Surely, this could not all be about Abe?

"Is Abe in trouble?"

Lieutenant Adams ignored the question.

I was beginning to get a better sense of her now. Thus far, she had intimidated, damned nearly scared the shit out of me without ever threatening to raise her voice. There was something haughty, aristocratic in her tone, although not a haughtiness to set one's teeth on edge. No, it was more that her certainty, her absolute lack of doubt which battered one into submission.

"Help me here," I went on, in hope rather than conviction. "I have no idea what's going on. How the fuck am I supposed to help you? Or Abe?"

The woman thought about this.

She sat back in her chair and glanced to Detective Inspector Danson who had been a mute witness – presumably an admiring bystander – as the young Redcap officer had verbally torn me to shreds in two minutes flat.

"I am not a professional detective like Mr Danson," Lieutenant Adams said. "I'm a psychological profiler. My job is not to catch traitors but to identify them. I characterise their patterns of behaviour. I give my superiors advice as to whom is dangerous, and whom is harmless. For example, the majority of your disloyal tendencies and resultant actions are harmless, with the notable exception of your well-practiced capacity to spin a tale, to contextualise an injustice whether real or false notwithstanding with equal persuasiveness. You are a man who might in another, less enlightened age, have spent most of his adult years incarcerated, or swung by the neck until dead at a sadly young age. In New Spain they might have burned you at the stake or crucified you, in Germany you would have been liquidated or sent to fight in one of the Kaiser's interminable small wars in Sub-Saharan Africa, in Russia you would have died of frostbite in Siberia building a railway or working in a mine or suchlike. Fortunately, for you, you live in a civilised country whose leaders respect the rule of law. Even today, accused mostly out of your own mouth of sedition, and suspected of conspiracy to betray your Monarch, you may rely on due process. Inevitably," she went on, as if she was a cat slowly drawing its claws across glass, "if the Empire is to continue to pursue this laissez faire attitude in cases such as yours, it must be well-informed. It must understand what it is up against. Clemency, mercy always has its price, Professor. I think that you are a very dangerous man."

I had no idea where this was going.

Every nerve in my body was saying: 'get up and run away; run through the nearest wall if you have to!'

"Me, dangerous? Seriously?"

"Ideas are much more dangerous than bullets, Professor."

I would have disagreed, except I did not. Disagree, that was. Lieutenant Adams viewed me like a Lioness sizing up her next meal.

"Tell me about George Washington?"

Oh shit!

I told every class the 'George Washington' story.

I wanted to get my students thinking, really thinking about what history was, how it worked and why it mattered. If kids wanted to learn a list of names and dates by rote that was fine by me but that was not actually learning anything at all. History was a thing that flowed through one's veins, that branched and died back, twisted and turned and was therefore, rarely predictable. The past tells you very little about the future but it tells you a lot about people.

"I don't use the George Washington story in the manner of a political polemic," I protested. "I use it as a thought experiment to encourage young minds to grow, to develop, to form their own opinions. To get young people interested in *our* history."

To my surprise, and consternation, the young woman smiled.

"So, imagine I am one of your students, Professor. Assume that I want to know if history is the autobiography of a madman or something that I, as a mere woman, can understand and that might, in some way I do not as yet comprehend, be of more than passing relevance to my normal life."

I fell for it. I was suckered in hook, line and sinker.

No fool like an old fool!

"If you live in some parts of New Spain history must seem like pages straight out of the autobiography of a madman," I observed. I thought I was being quite pithy but I got the same 'new student' look I always got.

In for a penny, in for a pound.

I was already guilty of something; albeit I had no idea what so with a sigh I started talking.

"I take what I do, teaching, very seriously. Our kids need to be taught well. When we send them out into the world they need to be ready for what's out there; that's what education is for. So, I have my own credo, as it were. And that's what I try to communicate with my students."

Neither of my executioners told me to shut up.

"I believe," I said, 'that now and then historians should stand back from what actually happened and why, and ask themselves what *might* have happened? It does not matter if one is a determinist or a fatalist; a believer in the great man (or woman) theory of things, or a conspiracy theorist, or simply a believer in 'what will be will be'. Frankly, there are points in the past where the world might easily have taken a different course. And no, I am not talking about chaos theory, whereby a butterfly flaps its wings and the world, in some non-specific, indefinable way is never the same again. Randomness and chance, the roll of the dice of death, birth, redemption, atonement or calumny are incalculable variables; that is a given. That is just life; c'est la vie. No, what I am alluding to is the possibility that there might be moments – perhaps, identifiable moments – when *something happened* that was of such *moment* that history thereafter took a radically different path from than that which it might otherwise have taken. That literally, in that moment the fate of great nations, of empires was changed by a single, decisive event."

"Hence the George Washington story?" Lieutenant Adams asked rhetorically.

"Yes," I nodded. "It is in all the standard histories of the First Rebellion but modern historians tend to underplay Washington's significance."

"But you don't?"

"No."

"I'm no student of mid-New England history," the woman admitted. "Tell me George Washington's story."

I was genuinely at a loss.

I thought I was being interrogated.

And still not sure why except it probably had something to do with Abe.

"What's happened to Abe?" I asked, doggedly.

Lieutenant Adams crossed her arms across her breasts, which were small, pert and generally proportioned in a most complimentary fashion to the rest of her personage. This I noticed because despite my advanced years – fifty-seven and counting, although the way things were going, not for much longer – I still notice these things. As Sarah would say, and Rachel, bless her, was also wont: 'Men!'

Okay, the woman was not going to answer my question.

She really wanted me to tell her the story of the Battle of Long Island!

'Can I stand up?'

This got blank looks.

"I always do this story standing up, it adds to the," I shrugged, 'atmosphere. It's not the same if I can't wave my arms around."

Lieutenant Adams waved for me to go ahead.

For a moment there was a look in her eyes that might have been a reaction to my surreptitious voyeuristically veiled – I hoped – scrutiny of her bust; but probably had more to do with which part of my anatomy she planned to order the torturers to break first.

'You have to imagine we're standing on Brooklyn Heights," I explained.

Detective Inspector Danson murmured: "that's about twenty miles to the west of here overlooking the East River and the bridge between Long Island and New York."

The woman frowned as she tried to sort out her geography.

"Is that north or south of the Admiralty Ship Yards at Wallabout Bay?"

"South."

"Oh, there," she sighed.

"The date is late on the evening of Tuesday 27th August 1776 and in the course of the day some nine thousand men of the citizen Continental Army – to all intents the only rebel army - have been driven back onto the Heights, which in those days were more high ground in open country rather than mountains of any description, by a British force of over twenty thousand professional soldiers including around eight thousand Hessian mercenaries under the command of Major General William Howe. The *American*, sorry, the rebels on the other hand are mostly civilian-soldiers. Among them are a number of sharp-shooters but man for man they are no match for the British."

I could tell Lieutenant Adams was impatient.

Danson, on the other hand, was a man who liked a good story.

But the lady was a woman in a hurry.

"The British already hold Staten Island and they have a fleet anchored in the Upper Bay well out of range of the guns guarding the Hudson and the East Rivers. The rebels had assumed the British intended to force the Hudson and drive north, splitting the so-called 'United Colonies' in half. George Washington, among others, had been so fixated fortifying and defending the Hudson that he had regarded the British build up on Long Island as some kind of feint. It was a classic case of two sides completely misunderstanding what the other regarded as the main objective of the campaign. William Howe did not want to conquer a hostile wilderness and spend the next couple of years mopping up the surviving continentals; he wanted to bring to action and to destroy the whole rebel army in a single battle. And by dusk on the evening of 27th August 1776, that was pretty much what he had achieved."

"Washington?" Lieutenant Adams reminded me.

"By that evening the continentals have already suffered over a thousand casualties and as many as half the regiments engaged that day had simply broken and skedaddled to the rear when the British charged their positions. The man who had been in charge at the outset was a fellow called Israel Putnam; although our friend George Washington had crossed the East River during the battle to see what was going on and ordered several more regiments to follow him before he realised how truly hopeless things were."

"Washington actually made things worse then?" Danson put to me.

"That's one way of looking at it. Anyways, the Continentals have been driven into defensive works with a more or less open flank in the south with their back to the East River and the Upper Bay. On paper there are as many as two or three thousand other rebels on Manhattan Island, but only a small proportion of them are front line troops, many are ill, not fit for service, untrained or required to man Fort George at the southernmost tip of Manhattan. And," I said, trying to be melodramatic as I began to pace – two steps this way and two back, time and again, "as dusk falls the British fleet, which has been awaiting its moment on the western side of the Upper Bay is preparing to set sail. On Manhattan Island they don't know if this is the long-expected attempt to 'force the Hudson' or to blockade the East River and trap the Continental Army on Long Island. To sum up the situation: one, the Continentals have lost the battle on land and are trapped; two, if the British fleet fights its way past the batteries guarding Manhattan and the western shore of Long Island ten thousand men – minus the thousand or so who have already been killed or wounded – will be captured; three, most of the Continental Army's senior men are on the wrong, Long Island side of the East River; four, if something is not done now everything is lost. But, one man has a plan!"

"This man George Washington, presumably?" Lieutenant Adams prompted, wearily.

I was not communicating with these people!

"Okay, I'm George Washington," I informed the two cops. "I'm going to tell you the way it is."

Nobody shot me so I took that as a green light.

"My name is George Washington," I continued. This was ridiculous but I had no idea what these people wanted from me except, most likely, my hide; so, what did I have to lose? "Like I said, it's Tuesday night and the last few days have been the most sanguinary of my whole life. I'm not a career soldier like Howe, Clinton, Cornwallis and the other generals on the English side. I'm a forty-three-year old Virginia planter who got railroaded into being appointed Commander-in-Chief of the Continental Army – which didn't exist at the time – the year before."

I had got to quite like old George over the years.

"My forebears were landed English gentry, my great-grandfather emigrated to Virginia in 1656 but my own wealth mainly derives from my marriage – a very happy marriage, I might add - to the widow Martha Dandridge Custis. I'm a tall fellow, some say handsome; despite my physiognomy being somewhat pocked by a brush with smallpox in Barbados in 1851. Physically, I tower over the majority of my peers. However, as to my military credentials, those are tenuous. My peers assume that I have been given my command on the basis of my Virginian 'connections', my 'commanding presence', and not a lot else and broadly speaking they would be correct. Back in the days when I was one of six ne'er-do-well surviving siblings of a merchant gentleman beset with financial embarrassments I had trained as a surveyor. That was back in the late 1740s and early 1750s. Frankly, although tiresome, the outbreak of the French and Indian Wars rescued me from my chosen profession in 1753. Unfortunately, not in a good way. My reputation was somewhat sullied in the action at Fort Necessity, and only redeemed when I accompanied General Edward Braddock on his ill-starred Monongahela Expedition. I would go so far as to say that my experience of *that* war taught me much of what I know now about *how not* to conduct military operations!"

I was getting into character now.

"Others had recognised in me characteristics and qualities of leadership that, frankly, I had not seen in my own person until I was offered command of the Virginia Regiment, a commission I held with pride between 1755 and

1758 charged with protecting the outlying districts of my colony against French marauders and their native confederates. I lost some three hundred of my one thousand men in the course of a score of trying engagements and skirmishes. To my chagrin I came to recognise that my superiors did not have a care for their men during the campaigns of those years. My Virginians were attacked by friendly formations during the Fort Duquesne expedition, suffering some forty or more casualties on account of the negligence of senior officers. Subsequently, I confess, that it was with no little relief that I hung up my sword in 1758 and returned to civilian life; never, I confess ever thinking to take up the profession of arms again!"

I shrugged, held my hands wide.

"But it was not to be. Congress called upon me to lead the Continental Army. I asked for twenty-eight thousand men; I was given nineteen thousand. We bested our enemies at Boston but I knew that the issue would be determined here in New York. Hence, I brought my raggle-taggle army south. My plan was to stalemate the English long enough for the winter to freeze the battle lines."

Detective Inspector Danson guffawed softly.

"And then what were you going to do, *George*?"

"I planned to lead my foes a merry chase. My men had no chance in open battle but our land is great and every man the British lost through sickness or in battle would take six months to a year to be replaced from Europe. I planned to let the predations of campaigning, sickness and war-weariness take its toll on my enemies. I'm not sure if that amounts to 'a plan' but on that last Tuesday evening in August 1776 it all seemed somewhat academic. As darkness fell it was likely that but for a miracle our rebellion was doomed less than two months after our Declaration of Independence had been promulgated at the Pennsylvania State House in Philadelphia. If our army was lost and New

York fell our enemy would surely hollow out the rebellion from within; without the Continental Army the British might strike north up the Hudson Valley or south towards Trenton and Philadelphia. It would only be a matter of time before the colonies were split in half, subdued in detail, or seized by the loyalist rump who sought to undermine their fellows at every turn...”

“Loyalists?” Lieutenant Adams objected, speaking for the first time in several minutes.

“Loyalists to the Crown. The war had set brother upon brother and friend against friend up and down the East Coast. I can tell you that dire thoughts rifled my mind that afternoon as I gazed out across the forest of masts of the hundreds of merchantmen, great ships of the line and the low, lean frigates of the Royal Navy waiting ready to unfurl their sails and force an entry to the Hudson and the East Rivers. I felt helpless, knowing full well that if the wind shifted, even a few points to the south of east or west, there was nothing in the World that would stop Vice Admiral Richard ‘Black Dick’ Howe’s men-of-war trapping my ten thousand men on Long Island. With the Royal Navy at my back and General William Howe’s – the British liked to keep these things in the family in those days, William was the younger brother of the admiral - twenty thousand mercenaries and professional Redcoats at his front, I would be trapped. Moreover, if the day’s fighting had taught me anything it was that I relied on my own generals at my peril.”

The woman vented a long, irritated sigh.

For the first time Danson gave his fellow cop a look that was very nearly but not quite, schoolmasterish. She shrugged, waved for me to continue.

“There comes a point in every campaign, rebellion, battle or whatever,” I explained, “when everything is up for grabs and Washington was general enough to know *that* time was coming, if that was, it was not already upon him.”

I slipped out of character.

"You see by then the war with the old country had been rumbling on for the best part of two years, Washington had driven the British garrison and the Royal Navy out of Boston that spring; but that was then and this was now, and the British had finally got their act together big time. The Howe brothers had succeeded in bringing over-whelming fighting power on land and at sea to bear on the so-called Continental Army of the fledgling, and barely united colonies of the East Coast. The Continentals were exhausted and Washington's guns were running short of powder. Out in the Upper Bay the guns of Fort Defiance on Red Hook, Governor's Island and at Fort George might hold off the English for a while but there were too many ships already in the Upper Bay and the moment Washington pulled men back from his defence works General Cornwallis's Hessian mercenaries – thousands of them - would pour through the gaps. Washington knew he had lost the battle and that whatever happened the British would be in Manhattan in days. So, he did what any good general would do. He took a deep breath and threw the dice one last time."

I resumed my seat at the table.

"Washington gambled, or at least we think he gambled; what seems to have happened was that he sent an order across the East River to Manhattan ordering every boat – effectively the local fishing fleet - to cross to the Brooklyn shore that night. He meant to mount a diversion and save as many of his men as he could before the enemy realised what was going on. It was his only hope. If he could keep his army 'in being' the rebellion might still have legs. It was a desperate move but not ill-considered. The previous night there had been a fog on the East River and the British clearly disliked fighting at night as much as his men; so, he might have got lucky. If all went well the evacuation would begin at four o'clock on the next morning, Wednesday 28th

August. It can't have been much fun waiting for the first boats to arrive. Periodically, English guns lobbed balls into the redoubts along Brooklyn Heights – Fort Putnam, Fort Box and Fort Greene – as Washington strode through the darkness, seeking out his generals."

I always thought of the George Washington fable as one long, convoluted shaggy dog story; the sort of thing one could drag out all night or conclude at a moment's notice. Most of the people one told the story to already knew the punchline so it was all about the twists and turns on the way, the journey not the destination.

"George's luck ran out around midnight. First the wind veered away from the north. First by a point to the east, then the south. For about an hour a fine rain began to fall, afterwards the clouds scudded inland to uncover the panoply of the heavens as the summer squall blew inland. Even by starlight the men on the shore could see the sails billowing from the top gallants of the ships of the line anchored off Staten Island. It must have been like watching one's death walking, very slowly towards you knowing that there was absolutely nothing you could do about it. Legend has it that a collective moan rose from the throats of the Continentals manning the redoubts as the English dowsed their cook fires and formed up to renew the assault at dawn's first gleaming, knowing now that their quarry was without hope."

The Battle of Long Island was a cautionary tale that ought to be ingrained into the heads of all young officer candidates.

"The Continentals had no control over the wind but by rights more seasonal westerlies would have blown Admiral Howe's fleet into the Upper Bay long since. But there's always the human element in the best tragedies; and that was supplied by Thomas Mifflin, one of Washington's commanders. Supposedly, he misunderstood his orders –

many of my colleagues in the history game think he was either a fool or just one of those men who misunderstand orders because they always think they know better – and pulled his regiment out of the line around the time the first boats from Manhattan were landing at Brooklyn Pier."

I sat back and studied my interrogators.

"Why the Hell am I telling you this stuff?"

It was as if Lieutenant Adams had been waiting for exactly this cue; she leant down, grabbed her attaché case and pulled out a battered book which she proceeded to place equidistantly between me and her on the table.

Oh...double shit!

This just gets worse!

The woman nudged the book towards me.

"Open it at the title page please, Professor."

I did as I was instructed.

I knew that I was not playing this thing anywhere near as calmly as I hoped I was.

"Please read *that* page to me."

"Er," I looked up, as if bewildered.

"Read it."

"*Two hundred lost years,*" I muttered. The book was subtitled: *"What the World might have looked like if George Washington had ducked at the right time!"*

I had to smile; I could not help myself.

"By a Son of Liberty..."

I made as if to thumb deeper into the book, which was old, dog-eared and smelled musty. The dust jacket had long since disintegrated and the front and back boards were scratched, scuffed and a little deformed, probably by dampness. However, the spine was relatively sound and it looked as if all the pages were still in situ...

"Please turn to page twelve, Professor," Lieutenant Adams put to me like a threat. "Start reading at the beginning of the second paragraph and don't stop until I tell you to."

Shit! Shit! Shit!

They would be taping this whole thing and sometime later today some goddammed voice expert would be comparing my voice with thirty-year-old tapes.

"Today would be good," Danson suggested tight-lipped.

I cleared my throat.

Remembered my mug of tea, took a couple of mouthfuls to wet my suddenly arid throat and to lubricate my larynx one last time before these comedians gave it a good stretch at the end of a rope...

"*George Washington suffered adversity with the cool dignity that he welcomed success. Reportedly, he re-assured his men that 'our guns will put those frigates in their place', waving at the Upper Bay. Hulks had been sunk in the East River and any warships foolhardy enough to brave sailing into Buttermilk Channel between Governor's Island and the coast would surely be roughly handled. But there were so many damned ships...*"

The words seemed familiar and yet strange; it was the feeling one sometimes gets looking at pictures of oneself as a child or as a young man when everything was different and the world so replete with possibilities.

"*Washington had ridden down to Fort Stirling opposite the southern tip of Manhattan to supervise the first companies preparing to board the boats now straggling across the mouth of the East River towards the Ferry Pier by the time he encountered Thomas Mifflin's men trotting down to the shore. He was aware that scores of men had already deserted the lines on Brooklyn Heights and had detailed officers to staunch the tide. Mifflin's men would not be turned back and on the high ground to the east the remaining defenders could clearly see their fellows deserting the defence works around them. Briefly, Washington's presence calmed what might have turned into a riot.*"

I made every pretence of having to read the text closely as if I had no idea what lay in the next sentence, paragraph, page or chapter.

"The first men were embarking on the rescue boats when the guns of the frigates Phoenix and Rose and the 54-gun ship of the line Antelope began to engage the forts defending the mouth of the East River. Six, twelve, eighteen and twenty-four-pound round shot began to skim through the helpless flotilla straggling across the East River. The first broadside, probably from one of the frigates raked Fort Stirling. At first the ships out in the Upper Bay took a battering but inexorably, they came closer and closer inshore, as if pressed by the weight of the big ships entering those enclosed waters behind them, duelling and subduing the batteries at the southern tip of Manhattan, on Governor's Island and Fort Defiance on Red Hook."

When I was a boy I used to walk across the nineteenth century causeway to Red Hook and explore the ruins of the old fort; the Royal Navy took over the island – more an isthmus now that so much land has been reclaimed from the sea around it – in the 1930s. I would stand on the rubble, gaze out across the Upper Bay and imagine the sight which might have greeted an onlooker as dawn broke that morning.

"The Antelope's foremast crumpled and went over the side but her captain merely anchored his command and, ignoring the fire from the gunners at Fort George – whose efforts were now much inconvenienced by the smoke blowing away from the ships and over the southern extent of Manhattan – poured a withering barrage into the men gathering, mostly cowering, south and east of the now smashed Ferry Pier. Meanwhile, on the heights the Hessians had carried Fort Greene by force majeure and everywhere the Brooklyn Heights line was buckling, splintering into a hundred, desperate close-quarter battles in which the part-time riflemen of the Continental Army were helpless before the bayonets of the British

Redcoats and the tide of German mercenaries."

The carnage around the wrecked Brooklyn Ferry Pier must have been indescribable. What might, wind and military competence permitting have been a classic evacuation of a besieged force under fire swiftly turned into a nightmarishly bloody rout.

"*It is not known at what point in the battle George Washington was dashed from his horse. As the sun rose over Brooklyn Heights the warships were so close in shore they were firing grape and chain-shot into the Continentals milling very nearly within hailing distance. 'Grape' was like being blasted by a giant shotgun with balls of buckshot an inch in diameter; 'chain' was what it said it was, chains attached to iron bars normally employed to rip up another ship's rigging. Suffice to say that the decapitated body of the Commander-in-Chief of the Continental Army was identified the next day lying some one hundred yards east of the site of the Brooklyn Ferry Pier...*"

I made a point of pausing and studying the spine of the book as if I was still curious about its title.

"I didn't tell you to stop reading, Professor," Lieutenant Adams reminded me.

I had not really bought any of that horse manure about her being a plain clothes cop with the Royal Military Police; she had the look and emitted the bad vibes more characteristic of the Crown's secret policemen, and now it seemed, women, too.

I had no idea what department she might work for.

I had been out of that game thirty years; ever since I hooked up with Rachel and as for the Sons of Liberty, heck, that was all ancient history like the Greeks and Trojans.

"*Unlike so many of his fellows the British initially interred George Washington's body in a marked grave somewhere in the earthworks of Fort Stirling. Some years later it was believed to have been exhumed and re-buried in consecrated ground associated with St Thomas's Chapel, a Lutheran house which once stood on the Old Jamaica Road but was demolished sometime in the 1870s."*

I looked up and met the woman's stare.

I realised she was older than I had guessed, maybe in her early thirties and she did not quite have the scrubbed and polished, unnaturally immaculate aura of a real Redcap

She nodded towards the book.

"The British did not call a halt to the bloodletting until the end of November 1776. By then three of Washington's five generals at the Battle of Long Island – Israel Putnam, Henry Knox and William Alexander - had been executed for high treason, Thomas Mifflin whose negligence had hastened the rout was a prisoner of war, as was John Sullivan who had been captured the previous day."

I suppose I ought to have been more scared.

"A lot more is known about the battle and the 'cleaning up' operations which went on throughout the rest of 1776 and the first half of the following year. King George III – German George as the colonists called him – wanted all the men who signed the Declaration of Independence, that 'heinous treachery', hung, drawn and quartered but much to his chagrin his ministers told him 'we didn't do that sort of thing anymore."

I stopped reading.

"From memory I think John Hancock the President of the Second Continental Congress was the last man to be hung." I grimaced: "I think that was only because his was the biggest signature on the 'heinous' document."

"Well," Lieutenant Adams purred like a cat toying with a bird with a broken wing, "as any woman will tell you, Professor," she went on smiling the sort of smile that made me want to wince, "size is very important."

Chapter 6

East Hempstead Police Station, Paumanok County, Long Island

Everybody had been on edge since the news of the shooting in the Upper Bay had come through. Whoever had taken aim at the King – over a mile away – as he walked on the quarterdeck of the battleship HMS Lion had been very good. The shooter had winged one of King George's bodyguards as he bundled his monarch to the planking.

Sarah Fielding had raised an eyebrow when she was told that King George and Queen Eleanor planned to go ahead with the 'planned itinerary' regardless.

"They think the shooter probably used a long-barrelled Martini-Henry," the grey-haired, heavy-set moustachioed man sitting beside her in the observation room reported, sotto voce.

"That's a bit old-school," she murmured distractedly.

"I don't know," her companion shrugged. "A real pro wouldn't take on a shot that long but a re-chambered Martini Henry with a 0.303 barrel-liner is still a good sniping piece."

The 0.50 calibre Mark II and Mark III had been standard British Army issue until the 1930s and retained by specialist units into the 1950s, mainly because of its reliability and its lightning fast trigger action. It was this latter trait which made the gun a favourite for hunters, and of course, snipers.

"They're sending a float plane out to the Lion to collect the round they dug out of the deck. We should know more by tonight," the man continued.

"I can't believe today's events are still going ahead?"

"The King and the Queen will be transported from the Lion to Wallabout Bay by one of the escorting destroyers. HMS Cassandra, I think they said. She'll take the Royal

Party across the East River when they're done at the Admiralty Dockyard and take them back to the Lion this evening. If anybody blinks at the wrong time the whole fleet will probably open fire!"

Sarah sighed.

"You know that *he* knows we're watching him, don't you?" She put to the man she had first met as a teenage cadet.

"Oh yes," he confirmed.

"Why are we watching him, sir?"

When the man said nothing she asked another, very pertinent question.

"What the fuck are those two clowns playing at?" This she asked waving at her husband's two interrogators.

My husband...

Well, strictly speaking that was not true. Isaac was a registered agnostic so there could be no church wedding and as they had never gone to a lawyer and signed a marriage contract their 'union' was of the 'common law' variety. Her 'legend' had worked surprisingly well with a 'partner' so deeply embedded in the lazy, complacent ways of academia. These days you had to work hard for a fellowship, literally do the hard miles and hope something turned up at one of the colleges one was 'associated with'; it meant living away from home for weeks at a stretch, and sometimes working 'out of colony'. Few husbands would put up with that sort of life but then Isaac was not the possessive sort and she had told him that she did not plan on having any children. Their 'marriage' would, therefore, be one of mutual convenience and basically, he got to sleep with a woman half his age now and then: what middle-aged man was going to turn down a deal like that?

Sarah still thought the whole thing had been a complete waste of time. Leastways, for her personally although not professionally because six months ago she had been promoted to probationary Captain in the New England Security Service.

Isaac Fielding had first been arrested in 1939; in those days nobody called student activism 'sedition'. He was active in student politics, involved in any number of protest marches and demonstrations. During that era all men between the ages of eighteen and twenty-seven were liable to be randomly 'drafted' into the Colonial Militias for service in the Alta California-Nuevo Mexico Border War; there was a lot of bad feeling about both 'the Draft' and the fact that the sons of politicians, rich merchants and whose families had friends in high places could, and often did, gain draft exemptions and or purchase 'substitutes' so that their sons were kept well out of harm's way.

The suspension of the draft between 1943 and 1955 had undermined the Sons of Liberty and ushered in a period of happy stasis across the college and university campuses of the East Coast and knocked all that stupid talk about a developing youth counter-culture on the head. Oddly the re-introduction of the draft, or as it was properly termed the 'Colonial Service Obligation' in 1955 had not been the trigger for renewed civil unrest many had feared. Possibly, because so many of the subversive mainstays of the still-born 'counter culture' had withered on the vine in the previous decade.

Nobody liked 'the draft' but most people accepted it was a necessary evil if the boundaries of the colonies were to be protected. Leastways, that was the way most patriots felt about it!

Back in 1939 Isaac Fielding had torn up his draft documents and thrown them on a bonfire outside the Governor's mansion in Albany. Strictly speaking, as he was still in the second year of his degree course at college in Buffalo he was de facto 'exempted from militia service' at the time, having only been issued with his 'draft card' in error.

Nonetheless, he was hauled up before magistrates, found guilty of disorderly conduct and defacing official documentation and given a six-month suspended prison sentence.

Later he was listed in Colonial Security Service files as a member of the New York Sons of Liberty, an anarchistic group whose name harked back to a secret society formed in the founding First Thirteen colonies in 1765 to fight taxation designed to pay for the then 10,000-man imperial garrison of New England. Its motto had been 'no taxation without representation', a colonial grievance not remedied until the early nineteenth century. The initial incarnation of the Sons of Liberty had faded away after the supposedly pernicious Stamp Act was repealed by the British Parliament in 1766, however, 'Sons of Liberty' had become, over the years a generic rallying call for misfits and malcontents who blamed the old country for all their own colony's woes.

Frustratingly, although the security services had long suspected that the Sons of Liberty – certainly in the East – had had a guiding hand, either a council or a single leader, it had proven impossible to penetrate the organisation's high command. The SOL more closely represented some kind of cellular free-masonry than the guerrilla or insurgent movements encountered elsewhere in the Empire; uncover one cell, or two or three and it made no difference, always, the trail ended where it had started. It was like chasing shadows. For all that it was an article of faith within the upper echelons of the colonial administration in New England that the Sons of Liberty was just the tip of a widespread conspiracy embedded in the very fabric of the American colonies; problematically, back in England they probably still believed the 'bumpkins across the other side of the pond' were crying wolf.

Sarah had assumed that Isaac must have discovered that she was a CSS plant by now. He would have kept her close.

The first rule of politics, life, war, anything was: 'keep your friends close and your enemies even closer.'

Judging by Abe's attitude – not unpleasant but distant – towards her he had probably realised, or Isaac had tipped him off, that she was not what she seemed relatively early on. Abe would have kept away from her once he suspected he was under surveillance.

Isaac had no doubt believed it was all about his son's little squaw up north; the respectable folks down in King's County had no truck with Indian girls and although the ordinances about the free movement of former slaves had been promulgated over a hundred and fifty years ago most blacks knew better than to move into the respectable middle-class settlements of 'the Island'.

Abe had been weird about that; as if he honestly believed there was something wrong with segregation and the ethnic purity requirements for colonial civil service and local authority jobs. Heck, even Isaac had tried to talk to him about the damage just being seen with a Mohawk girl in Albany was doing to his future prospects. Everybody understood a boy sometimes went with a native or a black harlot, that was usually accepted provided he did not brag about it in polite company.

But marriage...

"He's good," the man at her side grunted. "You've got to wonder what sort of a man can keep the sort of secrets he must have in his head from his own wife?"

Sarah felt the heat rise in her face, she turned bristling in offence.

Colonel Matthew Harrison raised a hand in apology.

"Don't you start getting het up at me Sarah Arnold, I didn't mean anything by that and you ought to know that by now." He had had reservations, a lot of them, about recruiting his goddaughter into the service. Truth be told there were moments he still felt a little guilty about it. That said, Sarah had taken to the work like a duck to water. She was a natural, sometimes he swore she could change her colours, chameleon-like, at the drop of a hat. "Just you remember I've known you since you were knee-high to a chipmunk!"

She was still frowning at him.

The old man tried to be emollient.

"Isaac Fielding has fooled everybody for thirty years, indoctrinated his kids so well they see a CSS agent coming a mile away. You stuck at it, how were we to know the man doesn't even talk in his sleep?"

Sarah's frown faded.

"I still don't get what they're," she waved at the window, "trying to achieve, Colonel?"

"If Isaac Fielding was going to give himself away he'd have done it by now. So, what do you think they're doing?"

"That book you mean?"

The old man nodded, ran his right forefinger across his moustache.

Recognition dawned in Sarah's face.

"Get him to read enough of it and then we can splice the tape any which way into a confession?"

"Yeah, if need be."

Chapter 7

Leppe Island, Montgomery County, New York

They had first come to the island in the middle of the Mohawk River south of the ruined settlement of Fort Johnson as seven-year old kids with their parents but not returned again until last summer. In the fourteen-year interval nothing had changed except, maybe, them and the world they now saw around them.

Kate had met him when he jumped down from the train yesterday morning – almost bent double under the two big sea bags he had brought from Albany – at the old deserted logging halt at Amsterdam. Even this close to the Colony's capital, Albany – little more than thirty miles as the crow might fly – the countryside was still verdant, much of it first growth, forested wilderness and he had probably been the first passenger to disembark at Amsterdam, a ghost town ever since logging and mining rights in this part of Montgomery County were returned to the Iroquois Nation twenty years ago, for several weeks. There were a lot of folk in Albany who still hated that even though, election after election, they voted the same racist Christian fundamentalists back onto the Colony's Legislative Council who had mandated 'separate development', or *Getrennte Entwicklung*, as the more extreme Lutheran sects insisted on calling the policy.

The tribes of the Iroquois Nation – nobody used the word 'confederacy' these days because that was a pejorative white man's classification – did not care for the reasons why. Cultural and economic detachment from the colonists, who were still viewed after hundreds of years as little better than opportunistic interlopers in the Nation's ancestral hunting grounds, had suited the peoples of the Cayuga, Mohawk, Onondaga, Oneida, Seneca, and Tuscarora tribes 'just dandy', enabling local chiefs and councils of elders to preserve the old ways, and to police and guard their own lands. Of course, young people exposed to the temptations of the colonial world outside the tribal lands by radio and television, dreaming of a life not dominated by the apparent tedium of the traditional hunter-gathering lifestyle, wanting to enjoy and experience all the benefits – no matter how illusory – of modern industrial and urban society, still drifted to the towns and cities of the south, or crossed the St Lawrence River into the northern lands where native Americans lived in relative harmony side by side with the European occupiers.

Kate had looked at the bags and frowned her 'all men are idiots' smile before she threw her arms around Abraham Lincoln Fielding's neck.

'If we put all that stuff in the canoe it will sink!'

This she declared breathlessly when, eventually, they got past the excitement of seeing each other again for the first time since Easter. That was when they had hatched their 'Empire Day weekend plan'.

'We'll have to make two trips,' Abe shrugged.

They had forgotten something.

He bent his face down to hers and they rubbed noses; just like the way they had, innocently as kids for all those years before they discovered that growing up, especially puberty, had a lot to be said for it.

Presently, they kissed.

Unhurriedly, breathlessly.

In Albany dating a Mohawk girl was well, impossible. Most of the whites automatically assumed a woman with a dusky skin was a prostitute or a maid, after dark a male member of the nation was liable to be rousted by the police or worse, brutally attacked by local bully boys. So, unlike other students taking his 'gal for a walk' down main street, or going to the cinema or more nefariously, taking her to a down town hotel where clients customarily booked a room by the hour, had never been an option. Moreover, everybody had heard about the college authorities and the police intercepting letters and hounding 'Indian-lovers' like him; so, inevitably, they had resorted to corresponding via friends, and occasionally trying to talk on the phone. Kate would wait in the tribal office next to her village's one telephone; Abe would go to a public call box and attempt to persuade a reluctant switchboard operator at the city exchange to put the call through. In the second half of the twentieth century it was beyond bizarre but that was what life was like in the great twin-colony of New York-Long Island!

'Have you been waiting very long?' Abe had asked.

'An hour, maybe.'

People said Kate – *Tekonwenaharake* – looked 'very Indian', very pure-bred, her bloodline visibly undiluted by the European invasion.

Even good people said a lot of crass things these days.

Whenever Abe looked into her dark brown eyes, gazed wondrously at her oval face, her slightly turned up nose, framed by a mane of jet black hair he was simply...entranced. She moved with a ballet dancer's lithe athleticism and when she was in his arms he was lost in her musky, pine-freshness, wholly transported out of the other reality of his life.

Involuntarily they both cocked their ears to the sky, alerted by the distant thrumming of an aero engine. The skies of the Iroquois Nation were unregulated, an oversight the authorities had allowed to go unamended because it meant 'decent' – that is, white – people were not troubled by the increasing overflights of the ever more powerful and noisy flying machines of private citizens and the military.

'Alex and I flew over this way last weekend,' Abe said.

Alexander, Abe's eldest brother did not really approve of

Kate but he had always been a complete gentleman about it, not so William, his other big brother. 'Bill' was a prick. Much though she hated to say ill of any of Abe's relations, Bill was a prick, there was no other word to describe him.

'The military are scrapping or selling off all their old aircraft. Alex got hold of a Bristol Model V – a two-man biplane fighter – that flies like a bird with all the guns and bomb racks taken off it.'

Alex had learned to fly when he was an officer cadet, done his time down in the borderlands of the South West and got a job as the secretary-training instructor at the Albany Flying Club. Supposedly, veterans like him were liable to a recall at any time after eighteen months in civilian life. Kate could not imagine that the thought worried Abe's brother in the least.

Alex had been teaching his little brother to fly the last time Kate had seen Abe. At that time Alex had given Abe a dozen flying lessons and while he had allowed him to land 'the kite' when they got back from one 'jaunt' over Mohawk country Alex had told him he was not ready to 'go solo' yet.

'I went solo for the first time about a month ago,' Abe reported.

Kate kissed him until they both came up for air.

'Is it really like flying like a bird?' She asked.

'No, well, sort of, mostly it's very windy and noisy!'

He burned to tell her how much fun it was to be in the air; and how bad he felt about lying to his brother about his – their – plans. Alex said he was a 'natural pilot' and had promised to 'get you properly qualified this summer'.

But all that would have to wait.

Kate laughed and for a moment, buried her face in the man's chest. There followed a short debate about why one of the two bags would be too heavy for her to carry on her own.

'*Rone,*' she declared, impatiently.

Spouse...

In the end he slung one bag over his shoulder and grabbed unavailingly at the end of the second bag as she hefted it effortlessly onto her back.

The Mohawk River had been in a somnolent mood as they had ferried the tools and bedding Kate had brought and the bags, the one containing a tent, the other clothes, tinned food, a small stove and two gas bottles, across to the island. Deep inside the trees they had spent most of the afternoon setting up their camp.

He had sat his final exams a fortnight ago. He knew he had breezed through the week of examinations after successfully completing that spring's trial practice term at the three-year old Queen Eleanor General Hospital Medical School.

He still felt a little guilty about going through the motions applying for – and being provisionally accepted for – a two–year post-doctoral degree course in the QE's already world-renowned Infectious Disease Control Centre facility at Churchill College. If things were other than they were in his colony, the world ought to be his and Kate's oyster. But things were what they were and there was no future for them together in the twin-colony.

They awakened that morning to birdsong and the rustling of leaves in the breeze, warm in each other's arms. There were still a few bears, wolves and no doubt wolverines in the forests of the Iroquois Nation. Not so many as in olden times although populations of species hunted almost to extinction by the white man had recently showed signs of recovery. Some of the older warriors spoke of mountain lions roaming the banks of the Mohawk but a few pug marks in the mud apart that was wishful thinking. Nevertheless, Kate had brought an ancient Lee Enfield rifle, one of those old pieces so popular in movies about the last Indian wars which fired a forty-five slug with middling accuracy up to about fifty or sixty yards.

Yesterday afternoon they had walked the island for about half-an-hour, satisfying themselves that nothing likely to eat or attack them was lurking, or had been in the vicinity lately. Prosaically, they were really only concerned in case draft dodgers or illicit hunters had holed up on their hideaway.

After they had coupled nakedly they had talked. They always talked in bed together, made love again, and talked some more. They had a lot of catching up to do, and stroking, kissing, tickling and just plain enjoying each other's bodies.

"Alex tried to talk me into flying down to Jamaica Bay to take a look-see at the fleet," Abe confessed. He had never worried about being a Lincoln until his mother had died, afterwards he had always written his name Abraham Lincoln Fielding.

Lincoln in England was where his mother's family had come from originally; that was in the post-rebellion influx of 'common folk' from the old country offered free passage and a share of the 'free land' expropriated from the families of the traitors of 1776.

His mother had attempted to bring up her children as non-conformists. She had had no truck with the Puritan wing of the Lutheran Church and believed that *Getrennte Entwicklung* was an abomination. What little faith Abe had ever had in a Christian God had died with her; for no merciful omnipresent, all-powerful saviour could possibly have allowed his gentle, clever, funny, patient mother to die that way after months of agony, the victim of an incurable, bone-eating cancer.

No, if there was a God and he was to be found in anything then it was in the natural world, in the forests and lakes of the virgin ancestral lands of the Iroquois Nation. Only the native peoples still retained their connection to and wonder for the marvels of the land in which they lived.

"I think my arm's gone dead," Abe murmured.

Kate rolled onto his chest, giggled and snuggled close as the pins and needles danced and burned up and down his right arm.

"*Rone,*" she whispered fondly.

Under tribal law – by rite and custom – they had been by Kate's father's consent man and wife these last three years.

"Wife," he sighed, holding her tight.

"I wish we could stay here like this forever..."

Chapter 8

East Hempstead Police Station, Paumanok County, Long Island

I am not quite sure when it dawned on me that I was being strung along – taken for an idiot, basically – by the good cop-bad cop, old-young, uncle-niece, ruthless-sanguine double act. I was not any kind of expert in Police or Colonial Security Service interrogation or prisoner handling protocols - I assumed I was thirty years out of date - but 'Lieutenant Adams' and 'Detective Inspector Danson' literally had no idea what they were doing.

I had not been cautioned.

Thinking about it, the desk sergeant had been going through the motions last night rather than nailing down every dot and crossing every 't'. The whole thing had a staged feel about it. Okay, my door had been knocked down in the middle of the night, I was not sure how I was going to explain how that fitted in with the 'being strung along' theory that was forming in my mind; but that apart, things just felt *wrong*.

I remembered Sarah screaming and cussing, then breaking down in floods of tears; she had never struck me as that kind of woman. I could imagine her squaring up to a cop and giving as good as she got, kicking and spitting as she was being dragged away. Just not going to pieces like that. Heck, she had been the one who had always worn the trousers in our 'marriage'. Well, when she was around; when you worked for the Colony School Inspection Board you travelled a lot...

"Carry on reading from page one hundred and seven, Professor,' Lieutenant Adams demanded, pointing at the book on the desk before her.

Two Hundred Lost Years. And on the frontispiece subtitled, I had thought at the time, cleverly, '*What the World might have looked like if George Washington had ducked at the right time!*'

It was never meant to be a polemic.

The whole thing was just an amusing satirical project; if the Lieutenant Governor of New York had refrained from using his powers of censorship to ban the bloody book it would never have attracted such a cult readership on the East Coast back in the day.

Written by: *Anonymous*.

Anonymous had become a *Son of Liberty* a couple of years later but I had had nothing to do with that.

I had destroyed all the drafts, my notes.

I had never even told Rachel about the book.

Over the years I had come across dusty copies of the damned thing in antiquarian bookshops, and nearly fainted with horror and pride when I found a copy of it in Abe's bedroom bookcase five or six years back. Since the 1940s the book had morphed from the dangerously seditious to the whimsically irrelevant; and yet now it was being brandished, albeit metaphorically, in my face like an accusation of high treason!

I turned the book around and pushed it towards my interrogators.

"Read it yourself," I suggested.

The way the man and the woman exchanged glances told me they were suddenly off script.

I sat back and folded my arms across my chest.

I confess I was beginning to feel a little bit silly.

"Do you deny that you are the author of '*Two Hundred Lost Years*, Professor?' The man who called himself Danson asked before he remembered he was not supposed to ask *that* question.

I thought his sidekick was going to kick him under the table for a moment. She tried to recover the situation.

"Your son is in a lot of trouble, Professor..."

"Why?" I asked. "What's he supposed to have done?"

"You know I can't tell you that."

They had played me for a sucker and I had not disappointed!

No fool like an old fool, and all that.

I looked over my shoulder at the mirror on the wall behind me, rose to my feet and went over to it.

"Sit down, Professor," Lieutenant Adams pleaded but she was out of character now and clearly a little afraid that she really was in a room with a dangerous enemy of the colonies.

I ignored her.

I knocked on the glass.

Rap-a-tap-tap!

It was weird how I had travelled from terrified hare in the headlights of an approaching car, stunned and meekly quiescent to irritated, straight to just plain pissed off in less than ten seconds flat once I had finally got my brain in gear.

Rap-a-tap-tap!

"Interview suspended!"

I recognised the voice which broke from speakers hidden behind the panels of the room's suspended ceiling. I recognised it even though it had lost the edge of youth, mellowed a degree. That Virginian drawl had lived with me over the years and deep down I had always known it would haunt me forever.

"The prisoner will be taken back to his cell."

I was not taken back to *my* cell.

Presumably, my old nemesis Matthew Harrison – in 1940 he was only just setting out on what had no doubt subsequently been a successful career in the Colonial Security Service of New England, judging by the fact he was the one calling the shots – had decided that the two stooges who had conducted my interrogation to date had served their purpose. They made themselves scarce as I was cuffed, bundled into the back of a Bedford lorry, hooded and dumped onto a hard bench for the duration of the journey to an inevitably less public place. There were far too many people to hear one's screams in a normal police station.

This time when my hood was removed I was in a windowless room possibly six feet square and the only bed was a concrete ledge along one wall. There was a slop bucket, otherwise the amenities were, limited. The air in the cell was on the cool side of not very warm even though it had to be around mid-day.

The cell reeked of stale urine.

My hosts had left my cuffs on and my hands were numb.

I was definitely getting too old for this shit!

I was having trouble focusing, too.

Great!

The bastards had put something in my tea back in Hempstead; nonetheless, I was convinced I was going to get to the slop bucket in time right up to the moment I didn't. I would have worried about the mess I had made a lot more if I had not blacked out soon afterwards.

Chapter 9

Shaker Field, Albany County, New York

"Tell me again why we're heading up to the north-west before we fly down to Jamaica Bay?" Demanded the shorter of the two men standing before Alexander Fielding outside the hangar which accommodated the offices of the Albany Flying Club. Alex was the shortest of the Fielding brothers, by a couple of inches to Bill and three or four to Abe – Ma must have fed his 'little brother' better as a baby or something – but his dapper, trim frame belied a natural whipcord strength which had made him lightweight boxing champion both years during his time at the Colonial Air Force Academy at the Patuxent River Air Station in Maryland.

Those had been among the happiest days of his life.

In fact, he had not known how much fun he was having until his eight-year short service commission had run its course. He had tried to re-enlist, that was four years ago but the New Spain border was quiet at the time so the CAF was mostly going into mothballs and his personnel file was not exactly spotless. In another couple of years', he would reach the top of the 'active' Reserve List, or if things got any hotter down south he could be back in the service any time now.

In the meantime, it paid to keep busy.

Barnstorming was okay; you ended up flying with a great bunch of guys. The down side was that you could get a reputation for being a wild man and the days when the CAF let 'crazy men' anywhere near its aircraft were long gone. So, three years on that circuit was enough. He had needed to look like he was 'settled', reliable when eventually the call back to the colours came.

The job at Shaker Field was a godsend.

Later Alex had discovered he had only got the job at the

Albany Flying Club because the uncle of one of his class mates in Maryland – Pilot Officer Frank Sinclair, who had been killed in a crash down on the border six years ago – had recommended his name to the Committee.

His predecessor had got a landing wrong in a Bulldog racer – the civilian version of the CAF's main front line scout-fighter at the height of the Border War – and before they could cut him out of the wreckage the fuel tank had lit off.

Bad way to go!

Alex's Bristol Mark V had been a CAF trainer throughout its fifteen-year service which meant it had probably had more than one bad crash in its time. The flip side was that because it had been in the service ever since it was rolled out of the factory back in England, the Air Force had lovingly repaired and cared for it. So, while it was not exactly 'new', it was, for an aircraft of its age, technology and vintage, a relatively well-maintained, reliable machine. Twenty to thirty miles an hour slower than a Bulldog, about as manoeuvrable, but much more forgiving with perhaps thirty or forty miles more range, it was an excellent basic trainer.

"I've never flown with either of you chaps before," he explained patiently. "Before I ask you to do any fancy flying I want to make damned sure that we are all on the same wavelength."

He was not about to take anybody's word for it that a man knew what he was doing until he had seen as much for himself *in the air!* In the flying game the quickest way to get oneself and one's friends killed was to take somebody's word for something.

"That's fair enough, old man," Paul Hopkins, the dark-haired, rakishly moustachioed twenty-four-year old son of a Massachusetts banker grunted with ill-disguised angst.

Alex had been warned that the man had been thrown out of the CAF at the end of his first year at the Academy 'despite his Boston connections'. The Hopkins were East Coast

Brahmins, the nearest thing to a New England aristocracy - many of whom claimed direct ancestry, like the wastrel CAF-washout standing in front of him now - from old and great European lineages. The senior echelons of the Colonial Civil Service and the Colonial Armed Forces were stuffed full of 'settler nobility', which probably explained why the border wars in the South West had rumbled on for decades. Well, that and the unwillingness of the King's government in England to risk a new general war with the Empire of New Spain.

"We're just wasting time and fuel," his companion complained.

Rufus McIntyre was a friend of Alex's brother Bill. He was a strange man to find in flying circles, 'churchy', introverted and mistrustful of most of the people around him.

Alex assumed this was because, like his brother, he viewed all non-adherents to his particular form of Lutheranism, or who did not physically attend *his* Church as a godless waster. Unfortunately, there seemed to be an awful lot of people like Rufus and Bill around these days!

No matter what their other differences – and they had had a few of those over the years - Alex had never fallen out with his father like Bill had. Bill had turned on their mother shortly before her death; practically accusing her of 'denying the Lord' her eternal soul. Still, with four siblings in the family statistically speaking at least one of them was bound to be a complete shithole!

That was Bill all right and his friend Rufus had the makings of a man cast from a similar mould.

"Sorry, chum," Alex declared, knowing arguing with the Rufus McIntyres of this world was God's way of telling a man there were some folk it was just better to punch on the jaw the first time you had the chance. "You're flying on a provisional licence issued by the Committee of the Albany

Flying Club and if you want to fly over regulated territory south of Montgomery and Albany Counties, I've got to certify, personally, that you are 'safe and responsible pilots'. So, what we're going to do is take-off, fly over Indian Country, do some formation flying, a few rolls and turns, nothing very demanding and return to Shaker Field. Our aircraft will be checked out and then all being well, later this afternoon after I've sorted out the documentation, we'll head down to Jamaica Bay. If you don't like it, sorry."

The rules were nothing if not inflexible.

If either of the other two men wanted to find somebody stupid enough to 'certify' them without seeing them in the air that was their funeral. Alex had no intention of putting his life or his job on the line for a couple of strangers.

"Bill said you'd..."

Alex cut off Rufus McIntyre.

"Yeah, well you can write what Bill knows about aeroplanes on the back of a very small postage stamp and," he was losing his temper, "if you're thinking, for a single minute, of trying to bribe me, forget it, chum!"

While Paul Hopkins had lost his sense of humour, McIntyre looked as if he was on the verge of physically attacking Alex.

Not for the first time the former CAF ace asked himself what he was doing 'accommodating' these men. He had planned to take his Bristol V down to Long Island that morning; press and movie photographers were always crying out for rides when something was going on in the Upper or Lower Bays. With all the ships assembling for the great Fleet Review tomorrow it was like Christmas had come early for the 'gentlemen of the press' and they all wanted a personal ringside seat.

A Bristol V was a perfect ride for a man with a camera, it was slow, steady, relatively safe in comparison to the higher performance Bulldogs and a lot cheaper to hire than the plusher, more comfortable modern aircraft, few of which had open cockpits these days. The real top-notch 'snappers' hated having to do their work from behind a tiny window in a pressurised cabin. The windblown splendour of a Bristol V's front cockpit provided the best seat in the house.

"We're paying you well, Fielding!" Hopkins reminded him.

"No, you're paying me what I could have made, easily, already today flying snappers over the fleet moored in the Lower Bay. I only took your commission because my brother asked me to!"

Life was never this complicated in the Air Force!

All Alex wanted to do was check out that Hopkins and McIntyre were competent pilots, sign off their papers and make sure they did not get lost flying down to the field at Jamaica Bay. What they got up to after that was none of his business. As for their little detour up into the Mohawk River country he had threatened to buzz his little brother's 'love island' and he meant to do it in style!

Alex was never going to be ecstatic about Abe and Kate – even though she was a really nice girl, and apart from being a pure-bred Iroquois, Mohawk or whatever, he would have had no beef about her tying Abe around her little finger. He was no bigot. He had nothing against the Iroquois Nation, as a kid he had had Indian playmates like the others – not Bill, of course, he had always been a first-rate prig – but that was when they were children and everybody had to grow up sooner or later. Heck, it was not even legal to marry a squaw in the twin-colony!

"If you want to fly 'legal' you've got five minutes to mount up and follow me into the air," he decided, obviating further debate. He was doing them a favour. If they expected him to kiss their arses too, that was their problem not his!

This said he turned on his heel and marched purposefully towards his Bristol V. His two unhappy 'wingmen' were flying almost identical Bristol VIs, theoretically a few miles an hour faster in level flight. However, since both Paul Hopkins and Rufus McIntyre had loaded what looked like enough luggage for a six-month stay on Long Island into the front cockpits of their aircraft they were the ones who were going to have trouble keeping up with Alex.

The Mark V was an out and out scout, the later Mark VI was a strengthened, and therefore several hundred pounds heavier, variant designed for a bombing role. Equipped with a slightly more powerful – but again, heavier – engine the latter's take-off and landing characteristics had never been as friendly as the earlier models.

He had suggested that they lighten their loads; leave anything they were not going to need overnight in Albany for safekeeping in the hangar. Bristols were good, sound machines unless you overburdened them; notoriously, the CAF had only ever recruited jockey-sized men as air observer-gunners on its Bristol IV, V and VI squadrons.

The two men had refused point blank to lighten their aircraft.

Alex had done his duty, warning them that once they filled up their fuel tank ahead of the flight down to Jamaica Bay their aircraft would fly like beasts, especially if the wind from the south west freshened that afternoon.

Leppe Island here we come!

Chapter 10

HMS Cassandra, Wallabout Bay, Brooklyn

It was daunting to think that the great Admiralty Dockyards complex ringing the bay with its half-a-dozen broad fitting out piers jutting out very nearly into the East River, framed by a forest of derricks and the rising walls of steel that were the two new fleet carriers Ulysses and Perseus – both still over a year away from completion – was nowadays, *only* the third largest in New England. It was dwarfed by the great combined fleet base and shipyards of the Halifax-St Margaret's Bay complex in Nova Scotia and back home by the yards on the River Clyde and at Rosyth in Scotland. Nonetheless, it still made for a mightily impressive vista as HMS Cassandra slowly picked her way through the flotilla of yachts and launches which had come out to greet the King that afternoon.

Several motor gunboats bristling with heavy machine guns formed an imperfect cordon around the destroyer; their crews' fingers never far from the triggers of their guns after this morning's 'incident'.

For his part the King had refused to make anything of the assassination attempt. There was no question of altering his and his wife's schedule; all engagements would go ahead as planned and that, was that!

Forsaking full ceremonial dress, he had donned his Blue No. 1 uniform, hardly the best outfit for a hot summer day in the colonies but as Eleanor was wont to remind him 'you never look more relaxed than when you are in your Navy rig'. This evening he would have to dress up like a proper popinjay; this afternoon he could get away without the antique tail coat and tri-corn hat, if not the oceans of gold braid his subjects expected of him. The main thing was that the brow of his heavily gold-encrusted cap concealed his stitched eyebrow.

'I am afraid we are going to have to use a gallon of make-up to hide *that* this evening, darling,' Eleanor had warned her husband as she inspected his turn out in the moments before they went up to the Lion's deck to transfer onto the Cassandra.

Unlike his father and his elder siblings, the Navy life had kept King George fit and trim, and cultivated in him frugal habits, tastes and moderation in all things. People were kind enough to say he looked young for his age; he preferred to think that any man fortunate enough to be seen in public on his wife's arm could not but be 'given the benefit of the doubt'.

Eleanor had stepped out of the shadows into the harsh glare of World publicity as if to the manner born. The expensive high couture she had previously shunned for modestly stylish glad rags more appropriate to the wife of a career naval officer, and the modesty with which she had insisted their children were raised – such things were relative since their offspring were princes and princesses of the greatest empire the World had ever seen – had stymied the Press and republicans at home and abroad. In retrospect she could not have cultivated the image of a normal, albeit well to do, English housewife and mother better, while quietly gaining a reputation for patronising good causes, mainly in the fields of education, child health and the affairs of the local diocese of Winchester, where the family had been based for much of the King's time in the Navy. Suddenly thrust onto the public stage she had blossomed, bringing an approachability and a new, human face to the monarchy and carried on being...*herself*.

Today she was attired in a calf-length grey dress, a single silvery broach above her heart. Regal and sensible her shoulder-length auburn hair was gathered in a bun beneath a hat with a half-veil and she wore matching, very nearly flat-heeled shoes. Her arms, and every inch of skin up to her neck were covered so as not to upset the vociferous East Coast puritanical lobby. Such things could be ignored later in the day when the schedule moved to Manhattan where the populous looked to the future not the past for its solace and inspiration.

Both the King and his Queen were a little taken aback by the positively Biblical throng on the quayside and everywhere they looked as they awaited their disembarkation. Literally, every vantage point was crowded. There were men hanging out of the cabs of the towering cranes, waving enthusiastically from the towering heights of the carcases of the two giant half-built aircraft carriers, packing all the adjacent piers, and cheering, swaying on the shores and hillsides in the middle-distance beneath an ocean of fluttering flags.

The royal couple had become connoisseurs of crowds, intuitive judges of their mood and to a degree, of their expectations. Their last trip to these shores had been over five years ago when they had spent over a month in New England visiting all bar six of the Colonies, journeying from east to west where they had boarded the old battlecruiser Redoubtable bound for the Sandwich Islands. Now they were on the first leg of a new tour of the Empire.

In all they planned to spend over six weeks in New England this time before again catching their breath in the Sandwich Islands – so fondly remembered from their last tour – before moving on to New Zealand, Australia, Singapore, Ceylon, and India, where they would spend nearly two months, ahead of traversing the Indian Ocean to the East African colonies, going on safari in South Africa, paying state visits to the Gold Coast and Nigeria, returning to the Americas to visit Barbados and Jamaica prior to *finally*, sailing for home sometime in January or February next year.

This time around HMS Lion, the cruisers Ajax and Naiad and six fleet destroyers, including HMS Cassandra would collect the Royal Party at Vancouver in mid-July, having taken passage in the meantime all the way down to Cape Horn and steamed back up to Canada, a distance of some sixteen thousand miles.

The Ajax and the Naiad had anchored in the Upper Bay a cable to port and starboard respectively of the flagship. Each was a scaled down version of the Lion, fifteen thousand-ton vessels armed with main batteries of eight eight-inch guns. At a distance their silhouettes were virtually indistinguishable from those of the four leviathans of the 5th Battle Squadron, in the same way that Cassandra's profile was yet again, simply a smaller, leaner version of the layout of the Fleet's great capital ships. That was a hangover of the days before electronic detection and ranging – ELDAR - was invented when confusing one's enemy's precision optical gun-laying had been the name of the game.

The King and the Queen walked serenely down the gangway to step foot onto the soil of New England to where the Lord Lieutenant of King's County – these days a purely honorific ceremonial post because re-organisations in the 1950s had concentrated all the real power in the hands of the Governor's Office – waited patiently, he and his wife both flaunting their old-fashioned plumage.

Lord Lieutenancies were sinecures reserved for retired senior colonial civil servants and worthies, their roles and duties a leftover from more feudal times which had tended until relatively recent times to unhelpfully blur lines of responsibility in the old Colonial regimes.

The King raised his cap to the tumult, belatedly remembering that he had promised Eleanor that he would refrain from so doing and thus frustrate any attempt by the serried ranks of photographers to get a snap of his 'war wound'.

Together they stood on the dock.

The ovation was deafening.

The 5th Battle Squadron's Royal Marine Band struck up *God Save the King.*

The Union Flag and red and white St George's flags out-numbered those of the twin-colony twenty to one. In the Upper Bay the three-inch saluting guns of the Ajax and the Naiad began to bark out the customary twenty-three-gun salute.

King George turned to his wife and said out of the corner of his mouth: "You do realise that all of this is for you, not me, my love!"

Eleanor, had threaded her right arm through the crook of her husband's left.

Now she leaned closer, smiling seraphically.

"Put your hat back on, darling."

Chapter 11

Leppe Island, Montgomery County, New York

Tsiokwaris had almost lost contact with his roots as a young man; going to work in the mills of Buffalo to send money home. His father had died in a bar room fight at the hands of a European several years before the restoration of the tribal lands yet in those years without hope he had sworn to live without the hate and remorse which had consumed the souls of so many of his childhood friends. Revenge would not feed his mother or his sisters; revenge was what got the angry young men of the Iroquois Nation buried in the ground before their time and their families condemned to live in the squalid, stinking shanties on the edges of the White Man's towns.

Revenge and alcohol were still the twin curses of his peoples.

Thirty years ago, 'separate development', or *Getrennte Entwicklung*, had begun to give his Nation back small parcels of its ancestral lands below the Canadian border; already, some among the White Man wanted that territory back, planting illegal 'settlements' around the fringes of Indian ground and then slowly, seeking to insidiously expand into the Nation's lands, stealing, piecemeal what they were afraid to seize face to face, warrior to warrior in war. It was hardly surprising that some of the young bloods chaffed at the caution of their elders.

'This,' they claimed, thinking as young people always do that they have the gift of perfect understanding over all things from time immemorial, 'is the way it began in olden times. First, they come as friends, then they rob us blind and move us off our hunting grounds. After that it becomes *submit to our will or starve!*'

It was not that simple of course, there was no Colonial

guiding hand in the illegal encroachment upon Iroquois lands; it was mostly the work of a few Christian sects and rogue businessmen and if the 'big men' in Government House in Albany were involved at all it was most likely only by association with a few corrupt, bad apples in their secretariats. In a funny sort of way, the men at the top in New England had as little time, and equal contempt for the mainly Puritan extremists and greedy opportunists scratching away at the otherwise – from its point of view – successful separate development policies of the last three decades.

Nothing that had happened in those years had undermined Tsiokwaris's belief that the way forward was through dialogue with the white majority. The entire surviving Indian Nation from the Atlantic to the Pacific comprised perhaps some twelve or thirteen million people, of whom less than a third still lived traditional lives. There were over a hundred million whites in the twenty-nine constituent colonies, protectorates and territories of New England, and south of the Rawlings-McMahan Line – which ran from Wilmington in the east to Port Oxford on the Pacific west coast for well over two thousand six hundred miles – was home to at least fifteen or sixteen million of the estimated eighteen million descendants of African slaves still living in the colonies. Hotheads talked of 'uniting with the black men' but that was never going to work; geography and arithmetic were too heavily weighted in favour of the White Man.

And besides, his old friend Isaac Fielding and his wife Rachel had taught him that not all white men – or women – were his enemies, and that good fellowship and reason could be, even if they often were not, the determining virtues of peaceful coexistence. Notwithstanding that the majority of whites were bigoted, ignorant of his Nation and its customs very few among them were bad people, it was just that they could not respect what they did not understand and they brought up their children to look down upon, and to despise 'natives'.

Tsiokwaris and his two nephews, both of whom had attained that adolescent age when his brother realised his first mistake had not been drowning them at birth, had waited in the trees until the three aircraft had stopped buzzing Leppe Island and performing acrobatics up and down the adjoining mile or so of the Mohawk River before dragging their canoes into plain sight and rowing over to the island.

His nephews had pulled faces when he told them that if they wanted to accompany him 'down river' they were going to have to dress 'Indian style' and travel light. But even modern teenagers could be persuaded to conform to a tribal *old fart's* wishes when it meant they could escape from their parents for a couple of days.

'No transistor radios!' Tsiokwaris had mandated.

The last thing he wanted was for his peaceful weekend to be ruined by the loud 'English music' – if one could call so much 'raucous noise' music – polluting the senses of the tribe's children. Already facing at least two days without sight of a TV set, panic had briefly creased the youngsters' faces.

The old man's daughter had told him where she and her husband planned to camp, tonight he and the boys would set up far enough away to ensure the young lovers' privacy was respected. Nonetheless, that afternoon he was looking forward to renewing acquaintance with his unlikely son-in-law.

The old man's daughter emerged from the trees as he hauled his canoe out of the water, from habit dragging it over stones not mud so as to leave no trace of his arrival in the mud to alert strangers to their presence on the island. His nephews followed his example and soon the canoes were hidden from anybody on the river.

Abe Fielding approached his second father with a broad smile and the two men embraced.

"I might have guessed you two would turn up!" he chuckled at his teenage cousins, both boys grinned and hands were slapped in the colonial way as if Abe was just another teenage confederate of the two youthful miscreants.

"You were right," Kate told her father as the group moved up the shallow slope deeper into the trees which covered well over ninety percent of Leppe Island. "The snakes must have killed all the rats."

Colonials killed snakes as vermin and wondered why rats and other rodents infested their towns and cities!

Truly the ways of the White Man were a mystery to the Mohawks.

"You guys watch where you are putting your feet," Abe told the youngsters. Every Mohawk used to know that unless you trod on a rattler it was going to go out of its way *to keep out of your way.* Likewise, you never put your hand down a hole unless you knew exactly what was living in it.

"You talk to your Pa lately, Abe?" Tsiokwaris inquired.

"A few weeks back," the young man replied with a shrug. He changed the subject. "I reckon that was Alex up there in one of those planes," he went on, chuckling. "He threatened to come up this way. He's going down to Jamaica Bay tonight. He says he'll make more in a day from flying photographers over the Fleet than he usually makes in three months at the flying club in Albany!"

"It must be quite a sight down there?"

Abe shook his head, his smile rueful.

"Some of the big ships are bigger than this whole island!"

Tsiokwaris had had his fill of big cities working in Buffalo all those years ago. He had visited Newark once but never Manhattan. One colonial city looked very much like any other; they all had a similar grid of broad streets at their heart and confusion and incoherence the farther one walked from the centre until at last one reached the sanity of the surrounding countryside.

He was tall for a Mohawk, five feet and about ten inches, with the taut musculature of a man some years younger than his sixty or so years. The brown in his eyes had faded down the years, and his long hair, now gathered into a single pony tail, was streaked with grey. In another age he might have been proclaimed Chief amongst his people; instead he was an Elder of his clan, one of a handful of men who spoke for the Mohawk in the councils of the Iroquois Nation.

Knowing that Abe wanted to seek her father's counsel Kate had led her cousins away demanding they catch some fish to 'earn your keep'.

The two men stood alone in the sepulchral quiet stillness of the woods, listening to the slow rushing of the river down the flanks of the island in the stream.

"I don't want to live a lie anymore," Abe explained hesitantly. "But..."

"What about your doctoral degree?"

"That's just a piece of paper, I..."

The old man knew where this was heading. The kids wanted to be properly married, to live as man and wife and if he understood anything about his daughter – she was a force of nature like her late mother – Kate ached to start having babies.

"You don't have to ask my permission," Tsiokwaris observed neutrally, "to take Kate away from here."

"No..."

"You've talked about this?"

Abe nodded.

"If we go far enough west, into the outlying territories, or perhaps right the way over to Vancouver, well," he shrugged helplessly, "we could live together openly. Without fear."

"Without fear," the old man echoed. "There's a lot of

frontier country between here and the West Coast?"

"We'd cross into Canada and take passage on the Dominion Trans-Continental Railway all the way from Ottawa to Vancouver. The other possibility is maybe going into practice at Winnipeg or Calgary, either way there's hardly any of this *Getrennte Entwicklung* nonsense north of the border."

The colonial settlement with the French and the native populations north of the St Lawrence and the Great Lakes was the consequence of an entirely different approach to that taken in New England. 1776 was one of those years that had a lot to answer for! Whereas, the British had wrested Quebec from the French only a few years before the rebellion they had not attempted to inflict a single colonial model on the whole vast, then largely unexplored country. The French in Canada had been assimilated into the Empire with their culture and traditions intact; in New England the 'English' way had been the *only way* and the ruthless brutality of the retribution meted out to traitors and to whole colonies had been every bit as savage as that suffered by the Scottish clans after the Jacobite rising of 1745. North of the St Lawrence River slavery had never been enshrined in daily life, nor the inflexible missionary Christianity of the first East Coast colonies.

There had been less poison in the system north of the border, less colony versus colony competition, thus, Canada was a nation in the making within the Empire while New England remained, and probably would be ever more, a collection of – albeit peaceably – warring colonies.

Canada was no kind of Heaven on Earth; but there was no law prohibiting marriage across racial, ethnic or religious divides and if he and Kate might have trouble finding a Christian communion which would marry them in the sight of Colonial Law, any magistrate or registrar could perform the ceremony and thereafter, Kate would be as respectable as any lady living in a great mansion or carried everywhere in a gilded carriage.

In Canada *their* children would be born legitimately.

Tsiokwaris's brows knitted for a moment and his eyes darkened.

He and Abe had talked of this day many times but still he ached for the coming loss of his daughter and his second son. He had suspected that this might be the parting of the ways; that within days Tekonwenaharake would be gone, her voice travelling through the wind of different lands.

When he and his 'son' had last spoken the discussion had been whether to leave this year or next; in his heart the old Mohawk had known the time was now it was just that he had not, nor would he ever, really come to terms with it.

The two men halted, faced each other.

"Does Isaac know?"

Abe shook his head.

"He's under Sarah's thumb and he's an awful liar."

The old man said nothing but he gave Abe a very odd look, one full of irony and oddly, gentle amusement.

"What did I say?"

Tsiokwaris shook his head.

"Nothing. Have you figured out what you'll do for money until you get settled where you're going?"

Abe nodded.

The Mohawk chuckled almost but not quite under his breath. He wondered if the boy realised that his common law step mother was not what she seemed to be?

On balance, no, he decided.

But there was no need to burden Abe with that as well, he had quite enough to worry about as it was.

Tsiokwaris walked on.

O, me oh my…

What would we all be without our secrets?

Chapter 12

Brooklyn Admiralty Dockyard, Wallabout Bay, King's County

Thirty-four-year old Victoria Fielding Watson sat in the crowded temporary scaffold-seating within less than twenty feet of the King and Queen. Notwithstanding she was seven months pregnant with her third child she had jumped to her feet with everybody else when the Royal couple had ascended to the launching platform – a stage erected under the bow of Yard Job Number 309, it was bad luck to say the name of a ship on launch day until the moment before the traditional bottle was cracked on her plates – and ecstatically clapped and cheered. She had been quite hot and bothered by the time she resumed her seat with the other 'senior wives'.

Vicky was fifteen to twenty years younger than the majority of the women around her. John Watson, her husband had lost his first wife in the influenza pandemic of 1958-59; and by all accounts buried himself in his work for over a decade before her arrival on the scene. A lot of the other dockyard wives had regarded Vicky as a gold-digger, although she had never been that. The fact of the matter was that she had liked – and felt a little sorry for John – from the first morning she walked into his office to take dictation. His long-time secretary, a formidable spinster who had been at Wallabout Bay for over forty years had finally retired, and Vicky was one of several 'temps' sent up to the 'First Floor' from whence the big men of the Yard ruled like not so minor princes and potentates.

John was under-manager of Slipways 3 and 4 at the time. For the last two years he had been Director of Operations for Small Ship Construction. This title was a misnomer because in Wallabout Bay terms 'small ship' simply meant any vessel 'small enough' to be safely launched from a slipway into the waters of the East River. The two big fleet carriers – Ulysses and Perseus - were, at nearly a thousand feet long and well over forty-thousand tons, being constructed in dry docks; but anything under six or seven hundred feet long and weighing in at less than twenty thousand tons still qualified as 'small', such was the scale of things in the great yards.

Vicky had not exactly made a beeline, or any kind of overt 'play' for John Watson. He was twenty-three years her senior, dapper without being especially handsome. However, once she had got to know him a little better she had discovered he was the most sensible man she had ever met and although he could be a hard task master in the Yard, underneath he was kindly, and very lonely.

She had made it very clear to him that she was not going to sleep with him until or unless they were married and he had greeted this with a smile.

He had kissed her brow: 'of course not, my dear.'

They had moved into his apartment at Fort Hamilton – which had had a marvellous view across the narrows of Hell's Gate which protected the Upper Bay to Staten Island – but the place had had too many lingering memories of John's late wife and after a year they had moved to a big house at Whitestone, a part of the Clintonville community set back about fifty yards from one of the estuarine tributaries of the East River shortly after Vicky produced their first offspring, Caroline Fielding Watson. They had since had a second daughter, Mary and they both hoped junior, who was kicking with excitement right then, would be a boy to complete their little family 'triumvirate'. Mary's birth had not been entirely straightforward so husband and wife had agreed that 'three' children would be a good place to stop.

Vicky had left the girls with Noma, their middle-aged Algonquian nanny and driven to Brooklyn with her husband where she had spent the morning mixing and gossiping with the other wives before trooping up into their grandstand seats to enjoy the 'main event'.

Of late the majority of the other women had finally accepted her, sort of, as a kind of 'little sister', treating her respectfully at least to her face. Vicky regarded most of the other 'senior wives' as sad old harridans but she had got used to keeping thoughts of that kind to herself. It might well be that in a few years' time, or sooner, that John would be ruling the roost, then all the old women would have to pay court to her!

In any event, Job Number 309 sat poised on Slip 3 awaiting her first introduction to the cold waters of the iron grey East River. Vicky's husband, having been introduced to King George and Queen Eleanor – my oh my she looked so elegant! – had slipped away to supervise what he liked to call 'the mechanics of the launching' from ground level.

The dear man invariably returned home from a launching with grime on his best suit, spots of oil on his tie and a shirt smeared with and reeking of slipway grease.

From Vicky's vantage point above and behind the launch platform she could see all the way down the port flank of the new ship. It was really still just an empty steel carcass. Although her fire and turbine rooms had been fitted out otherwise she was a shell waiting to be filled. A temporary mast had been raised amidships between where her two raked-back smoke stacks would eventually stand, from whence a giant Royal Standard flew proudly in the breeze.

John had told her that the ship was the first of a new class. Originally laid down as an eight-gun light cruiser – a scaled down version of the 'heavies', the Ajax and Naiad anchored out in the Upper Bay – she was to be completed as a so-called 'hybrid anti-aircraft platform'. This meant that she would be equipped with four 55 calibre BL 6-inch Mark XXX guns mounted in two twin turrets – identical to those which made up the Lion class battleships' secondary batteries – forward of the superstructure. The aft third of the ship had been modified to mount twin twenty-feet high launch rails for the new, still experimental XB-293 two-stage long-range Seafire guided missile.

Everything to do with the Seafire system was highly classified, so secret that once the new ship was fitted out she was scheduled to sail to Scotland where the first prototypes would be loaded and tested. Today the launch 'rails' on the cruiser's stern were plywood, for show. However, now that Vicky had seen the scale of those 'rails' it was obvious that the Seafire must be a monster of a rocket!

Work elsewhere in the Dockyard had ceased at mid-day ahead of the arrival of HMS Cassandra bearing the Royal couple. Normally, at this hour the shadow of the towering King Edward VI Manhattan Bridge – carrying the road from Long Island on its top level, and the two railway tracks across the East River - began to encroach on the western edge of the Wallabout complex but the sun had gone behind gathering clouds.

With the murmuring of the crowd stilling Vicky heard the clatter of a train rolling high over the river. The great structure – the original, by modern standards, ridiculously over-engineered wrought iron construction was nearly a hundred years old, the roadway having been added only five years ago – had been designed to allow the tallest sailing ship free access to the East River. Even now, the great ELDAR masts and aerials of one of the Lions could easily pass beneath the central span. In the last century there had been plans to span the Hudson River also; it had never happened. The money had run out and people had been complaining ever since about how it would have been much more rational, and certainly a better investment, to bridge the Hudson first.

The past is indeed a strange country!

What might have become of a quiet, out of the way little port city like Manhattan if it had been linked to the mainland via a second King Edward VI bridge?

Instead, the business and financial centre of affairs had moved north to Albany and Buffalo, leaving quaint little 'New York', effectively Manhattan-Brooklyn as a cargo depot and shipyard, and Long Island as the place tens of thousands of well to do colonists came to spend their summers and to sail their boats. Not that Vicky was complaining; the unfortunate souls condemned to live in the sprawling urban wildernesses of Albany and Buffalo were welcome to their 'city life', at least down here in the south the roads were not constantly gridlocked, and crime was virtually unknown outside the tenements crowding around the Dockyard district. Personally, she had no time for those who constantly wanted to churchify Long Island; the village where she lived, Whitestone, was perfectly all right the way it was and if those blasted Puritans had their way the summer vacation business - the only thing keeping many isolated rural and coastal communities economically viable - would go elsewhere. That apart, she honestly believed that she lived in the best place in the colonies to raise a family.

The Lord-Lieutenant of King's County had stepped up to the microphone sited beneath the bow of the new ship.

The launching ceremony was about to begin.

There were spits of rain in the air.

Chapter 13

East Islip, Suffolk County, Long Island

From the stench I concluded that I had probably been sick on myself and pissed myself for good measure.

It was several more seconds before I worked out that I must have been revived by the frigid contents of a bucket of cold water. Initially, my head hurt so much I guessed I might have been hit by the bucket as well as its freezing contents.

My hands were cuffed behind my back, the chain looped through the back of the chair I was sitting in. Or rather, that I was slumped and generally lolling about in. I desperately tried to focus my eyes on something to make the nausea go away.

I am definitely getting too old for this shit!

SLAP!

I did not see it coming.

SLAP!

I felt my nose running.

Blood?

Or just the water still draining off my head?

"I've been wanting to do that for months!"

I blinked dazedly up at my wife.

"That figures," I muttered.

I thought Sarah was going to slap me again.

I knew she wanted to.

Oh well, at least we were not going to have to go through a protracted trial separation or divorce.

Every cloud is supposed to have a silver lining but this is going a bit too far...

I suppose that it is at times like this: that is, later, much later in a day that began with one being dragged out of bed in the small hours of the morning with a gun at one's head, a day playing mind games with the police which had carried on going down-hill, and reached an apparent nadir when I was drugged, had passed out and messed myself, and finally, regained consciousness hand-cuffed to a chair with my ex-wife conducting affairs with the flat of her right hand, that a chap is, quite naturally, liable to feel a tad hard done by.

I confess, I was a bit down in the dumps.

Sarah was dressed up in the green uniform of the CSS. She had captain's crimson tabs on her lapels and I could tell that her calf-length skirt was tailored to flatter her figure.

I decided that the only thing to do was to imagine her naked.

Sarah was a lot less scary when she was butt naked.

Not to mention a sight for sore old eyes.

I gave her what I hoped looked like a lopsided grin: 'Was it something I said, sweetheart?'

She obviously did not see the joke which given the circumstances – I was the one handcuffed to a chair in what looked like a disused changing room – lacked a certain style.

A changing room...

I could see where the benches had been along the white-tiled walls, underfoot there were a couple of drain holes covered by rusty grills and I thought I glimpsed the edge of what might have been the communal after match bath beyond Sarah's shoulder.

I recollected that there was a derelict football stadium down by the estuary of the Connetquot River. Most of the locals would have translated the old Algonquian name as 'great river'...

My mind was wandering.

"What in God's name did you comedians put in my tea?" I inquired.

It seemed like a reasonable question.

I was still trying to figure out why Sarah had just taken

a step to the left when the next bucket of icy water drenched me.

"Oh, very funny," I spluttered. Quite feebly, thinking about it.

"You're going to tell me everything," she replied.

Okay, it was good to talk.

That was where most marriages went wrong; the parties stopped talking to each other.

"Er, about what?"

"The plot."

"What plot?"

SLAP!

Well, that only goes to show you: I thought I was married to a south paw and then out of the blue she finds a stinging right cross! Perhaps, we ought to have talked more?

I shook my head until the ringing in my ears went away.

"Ouch," I complained.

All things considered I did not want to do anything likely to piss her off so badly she called in a man to do her woman's work. Shapely as Sarah might be she was a lightweight chastising me with the flat of her hand – well, hands – not a middleweight balling his fists.

"I know it's a wife's prerogative to have her husband at a disadvantage from time to time but this is beyond weird..."

She stepped behind me.

Whispered in my ear: "You talk in your sleep, *husband*."

I wondered if I ought to tell her she *snored* in her sleep some nights?

No, no, perhaps on balance this was not the right time.

"I'm hardly likely to remember what I say," I remarked.

"I know everything."

"Wives do," I agreed.

I could smell her hair, feel her lips by my ear.

It was almost erotic...

If the literature was to be believed – scientific literature,

I mean, not the sleazy top shelf magazines fellows of a certain ilk used to be able to buy in the twin-colony before the bloody Puritans took over - there were a lot of men willing to pay good money to be tied up, abused and slapped about like this. I had never seen the point of it myself but viewed from a certain angle, and assuming a certain mindset, I could see how a dirty old man like me might get a rise out of it...

SLAP!

For me the slapping rather spoiled it.

I think my head must have hit the floor when Sarah pushed me and the chair over because the world went black momentarily, or for a long time, I had no idea which.

Chapter 14

Brooklyn Admiralty Dockyard, Wallabout Bay, King's County

Queen Eleanor patiently awaited her turn. First the Superintendent of the Brooklyn Admiralty Dockyards gave his speech of welcome, extemporising somewhat until he received the signal that the final preparations for the launch had been completed.

'It is always a fine judgement about how many of the restraints and blocks to remove or knock away, and how many of the tackles to loosen off to ensure that when the bottle actually cracks on the bow of the vessel that the ship can actually be safely launched down the slipway by the simultaneous removal of the last critical restraints,' her husband had once explained to her. 'It is damnably easy to inadvertently launch the blasted thing early and then one looks like a right dunce waving at the ship floating half-a-mile away in the water!'

The Brooklyn Yard had mounted the bottle of Virginia Champagne – not a very good vintage, thank goodness – on a mechanical arm which upon her pulling the appropriate lever would prescribe an eighty-five-degree downward arc before exploding on contact with a six-inch sharpened 'rib' welded to the hull for this purpose. This was a huge relief to Eleanor because the first time she had attempted to launch a ship the bottle had not broken even though the glass had been half sawed through prior to the event.

The bow of the cruiser soared some ten feet over her head.

The ship's sharp stem was literally beside her, close enough to touch without fully extending her arm.

The public-address speakers boomed and echoed.

Some seventy yards to her right the mighty steel sarcophagus of HMS Perseus was rising out of the depths of the giant dry dock, between the Polyphemus and the aircraft carrier the keel of the second ship of her class was already laid, a skeleton of steel rising from the slip. To the left of the looming bow lay the ungainly, slab-sided hulls of two assault ships – odd vessels with huge internal docks which could be flooded down to allow each to discharge their cargo of landing craft – both due to be launched in the coming months.

'The thing is that once they give you the nod, not to hang about, my dear,' her husband had advised the Queen the first couple of times she had done this. 'Once they've got the ship primed to slide a strong breeze can set the thing off. So, stepping lively is the order of the day!'

"Pray stand for Her Majesty the Queen!"

Oh, the colonials were so sweet!

Everybody knew that she was only Her Royal Highness, Princess Eleanor and not really Her Majesty but the farther one was from London the more sensible people became she had discovered on her travels. Although she always missed England when they were away on one of their 'Grand Tours' she invariably came home refreshed and somehow, with her faith in the peoples of the Empire restored.

"Here! Here!" She heard her husband guffaw enthusiastically. She had been and forever would be his Queen.

Eleanor stepped to the battery of microphones.

Her hand rested lightly on the lever which would set things in motion.

"It is with enormous pleasure that my first act upon setting foot at my husband's side on the proud soil of New England is that I should be asked to launch one of the Royal Navy's most modern ships."

There was the inevitable temptation to milk the expectant quietness that settled at a moment such as this. She had sent battleships on their way, and bigger cruisers than the one before her now. However, the thrill of setting so many thousands of tons of steel sliding down into the water was the same regardless of the size of the ship.

She was breathless.

Composing herself she gripped the launch lever tightly.

"It is with immense pride and with all my heart that I name His Majesty's Ship Polyphemus. And in launching her upon her career I wish all who sail in her good luck and cheer!"

She tugged at the launch lever.

It stuck.

In a moment Eleanor's husband had stepped beside her, waving at the crowds and nonchalantly snapped the 'sticky' handle down. To all the world it would have seemed that he had simply moved beside his wife to get the best view and to savour the moment.

The bottle smashed into a thousand pieces against the flank of the cruiser.

Nothing happened.

However, this was not uncommon.

There was over eight thousand tons of deadweight sitting on the slipway and when the last blocks were hammered away inertia was governed not by the will of mere men but by the physical laws of the Universe.

Sometimes it took a second or two, on other occasions several. Ships had been known to 'stall' for minutes, or in extremis, hours before, with miniscule, imperceptible momentum beginning to move.

HMS Polyphemus sat in her starting blocks for one, two, three, four, five seconds by which time the launching party was beginning to get nervous.

"Shall we give her a push, my dear!" King George suggested to his Queen.

"Yes, why not!"

Their voices carried over the speakers around the

Brooklyn yards and stirred a wave of clapping and cheering.

Together, the King and Queen put their hands to the cold metal of the cruiser's bow at the very moment she began to slide.

Eleanor felt the ship moving away.

It was all she could do not to give her husband a huge hug in unlikely girlish delight; and from the broad smile on his face and the laughter in his eyes he was similarly moved. Decorum forbade such a 'scene' in public, more was the pity!

Slowly, slowly, then with unstoppable inevitability HMS Polyphemus slid stern first towards the waters of Wallabout Bay. It was the cue for clouds of confetti and streamers to be launched into the air. On the quarterdeck of HMS Cassandra, the destroyer's two-inch saluting 'pop gun' began firing into the air. The Admiralty Dockyard Band struck up a raucous march.

'The other thing about launching a big ship is that once it starts moving the only thing that is going to stop it is the water and hundreds of tons of chains,' Eleanor's husband had pronounced all those years ago when he, and she, had been unexpectedly catapulted into Buckingham Palace.

The King had put his arm about his wife's waist, and she his; everybody was watching HMS Polyphemus so protocol and stupid conventions be damned!

The cruiser was gathering speed.

Rushing to embrace her natural environment.

She had slid at least one hundred and fifty feet by then.

Some witnesses later claimed the explosion had come from within the mid-section of the cruiser; actually, it had occurred on the slipway, beneath the shallow bulge of her starboard flank as her turbine spaces were passing above it.

There was a small bang at first; momentarily followed by a much bigger detonation which showered the workers and their families lining that side of the slipway with a blizzard of red hot shrapnel and debris.

Instantly, there was pandemonium.

The ship kept sliding, faster and faster; nothing could stop her. Not even the wrecked slipway nor the jagged crater edges over which the whole forward hull of the Polyphemus lurched and juddered as she began to topple, inexorably onto her starboard flank as she raced down to the cold waters of the East River.

The dreadful screech of rending metal, of whole compartments within the hull disintegrating, twisting, collapsing would live with those who witnessed the terrible spectacle of the cruiser slowly falling over onto its right side as she went into the water.

The most frightening thing was the speed with which the disaster had happened.

From the ship starting to move to her coming to rest, on her starboard side slowly sinking into the relatively shallow, muddy bay could not have taken more than thirty seconds. In that time over half the men onboard her – Polyphemus's launching crew – some forty men and as many lining the slipways had been killed and perhaps two hundred others injured, many severely.

In less than a minute the cruiser's stern had settled on the bottom, her bow and port side proud of the lapping waves.

From her vantage point in the stand behind the launching platform Victoria Watson had watched the tragedy play out with numb horror.

She had seen the King take his wife in his arms; yell at his bodyguards to: "Protect the Queen!"

And then the Royal couple had been hustled away.

Now she stared in stunned disbelief at the sinking wreck little more than four hundred yards away and knew that her life would never be the same again.

She was married to the man *they* would never forgive for having allowed *this* to happen.

It was cruel and unjust but it was the way of the World.

Her good life had just come to an end and right then it felt as if the sky was about to fall on her head.

She gasped as a sharp pain doubled her over.

Suddenly, the other wives were all around her.

"Vicky, are you all right?"

Chapter 15

Leppe Island, Montgomery County, New York

The spring floods had piled a stony beach at the northern end of the island and Abe, Kate, Tsiokwaris and his nephews had sat around an open fire eating the fish the boys had caught that afternoon and talking in low tones long into the evening. It was a special night for they all knew that tomorrow their worlds would begin to change forever.

'Tomorrow is Empire Day. The White Man's most holy day,' Kate's father had prognosticated sagely. 'When better to begin to be invisible?'

Abe had mulled this over.

"You went very quiet, husband?" Kate asked as they picked their way back through the trees to their tent.

Other than his brother Alex, nobody knew where Abe was. The men with whom he shared lodgings in downtown Albany knew he was away until the middle of next week; they thought he had gone home to Long Island. There was no particular reason to leave for Canada now, or even in a year's time; except that he had already lived too long in a country in which his soul and his mortal conscience would forever be unquiet.

"We can never have the life we want or deserve in this land," he murmured, squeezing her hand. "Black Raven is right. We should go now. Not wait for another few days. We'll only get frightened again and put it off."

They had talked of leaving many times.

Planned for that day.

Even this time they might have lost their courage.

"Tomorrow we start our new life," he said.

Once he was formally awarded his Diploma permitting him to practice medicine in the Colony of New York-Long Island he would be indentured to the Colonial Office for five years in payment of his tuition costs. He could be sent anywhere. In the event he obtained a post-graduate position his indentured service would simply be deferred, extended by another two years. Whereas, if he left now the Colony had no legal recourse, other than to add his name to the Colony's 'Draft List' for service in the militia, and he sure as Hades was never going to go fight for the oil men trying to steal the black gold of West Texas from New Spain.

That was what the Border War had always been about.

Oil, and whatever gold and silver was buried in the mountains of California, not to mention the lumber of the forests of the Oregon Territory and the great natural port of Sammamish, New England's one Pacific-facing city port. All those things had only ever mattered to the Colonies, not to the great men of Empire back in England - to whom Vancouver and the coasts of British Colombia was gateway enough to the Pacific - which was probably why the Border War with new Spain had never spread beyond the Americas.

If Abe was being cynical about it, the fact that the Colonies voluntarily maintained a large standing army to threaten the Spanish on their south western borders saved the exchequer in England untold millions of pounds ever year in garrisoning costs the British taxpayers probably did not want to pay.

Whatever...

He had no intention of becoming involved in that particular imperial game!

So, they would leave now.

"Good," his wife whispered.

They shed their clothes in the warm darkness beneath the canvas and squirmed into each other's arms. Kate giggled and reached down for him as she rolled onto her back.

"We don't need to be careful anymore," she sighed in a way that instantly trebled the blood supply to his already engorged member and incited his libido to spontaneously combust.

Careful was a thing they had always been apart from the first time they had coupled. That had been a frantic, needful thing when they had both been only fourteen which had scared the living daylights out of them when the red heat of the moment had passed. They had been very lucky. Thereafter they had been *very, very* careful; abstaining from penetrative intercourse other than at ultra-safe times of the month – Kate's aunts were a font of sound advice on such things when she was younger – and Abe, for his part had tried his best to withdraw at the 'right moment' although sometimes he got carried away...

In the Crown Colony of New York-Long Island it was illegal to sell condoms to persons under the age of twenty-one; and several religious groups were actively lobbying to ban their sale altogether. So, getting hold of 'French letters' had always been problematic. The First Thirteen colonies stuck together on most things but none so righteously as the 'contraception issue' and 'abortion', meaning that there were an awful lot of illegitimate, unwanted children in orphanages up and down the East Coast.

From Abe's medical training he knew that the 'condom problem' – that is, the restricted availability of the same, was one of the main causes of sexually transmitted diseases in the general population, second only to men either carrying, or suffering from STDs returning from 'the border' and from other service with the militia 'out of colony'.

The trouble was the religious bigots always had the last say whenever anybody put a rational public health case before the Colonial Legislature supporting colony-wide limited 'birth control' and rational 'public sexual health' measures. It was ridiculous. Back in the old country they had had rigorous legislation in force for over a century mandating health checks on everybody entering the country, and basically, adopted a liberal approach to questions of population demography – a code word for birth control – and the right to life issue, in other words, regulating abortion not banning it outright. Overall public health in the old country was therefore, not unsurprisingly better than it was in new England with average life expectancy in England, if not in Wales and Scotland – being five to six years higher than in the East Coast Colonies.

Anyway, he and Kate had always tried to be *very* careful.

But they did not have to do that anymore.

She moaned softly as he sank into her.

They kissed, wetly, lazily.

She wrapped herself about him as he rose and fell on her; clung to him when he was spent, gloriously impregnating the woman he loved with every exquisite spasm.

Chapter 16

HMS Lion, Upper Bay, New York

The Governor of the Crown Colonies of the Commonwealth of New England, Edward Philip Cornwallis Sidney, 7th Viscount De L'Isle, who used his full title 'The Lord De L'Isle, Dudley and Northampton' in his annual appearances in the House of Lords to make his customary report on the year just completed in the Americas, was still attired in his full ceremonial regalia. Minus his plumed hat which he had thrown down on the table in the King's stateroom shortly after his arrival onboard thirty minutes ago.

The King had politely detached himself from his travelling court – about a dozen advisers, retainers and ladies in waiting who together formed the Royal couple's peripatetic 'kitchen cabinet' – after having taken general soundings about how the day's events impacted on tomorrow, and the coming weeks' engagements.

Decisions needed to be taken.

"Bertie," the Governor of New England appealed in exasperation, "this is absolute madness. Some bloody 'patriot' with a long sniper rifle took several pot shots at you while you were having your morning cigarette on the quarterdeck this morning," he went on, pacing irascibly.

Fifty-nine-year old De L'Isle still cut a lean, albeit stiff figure of a man in his ceremonial finery; very much the former, athletic sportsman who had rowed victoriously for Oxford in the Boat Races of 1937 and 1938, and served with immense distinction in either three, or four – the King forgot the exact number, and knew his old friend probably had too – small wars with the Grenadier Guards before laying down his sabre and signing up with the Colonial Service.

"Eleanor, can't you talk some sense into Bertie?"

De L'Isle was not only a life-long friend to the King and

Queen, he was family also. He was a second cousin to the King and first cousin to the Queen, whom he had known since they were both very young children.

Eleanor's parents had been horrified when Philip De L'Isle had married the younger daughter of a General, a mere 'honourable', out of 'love, for goodness sake!' They had had high hopes of a match between the gallant young cavalry officer who had inherited his father's ancient titles at the impossibly young age of twenty-two while still unmarried, and Eleanor's older sister, Antoinette.

De L'Isle's wife, Elizabeth, by whom he had sired a brood of four sons and two daughters – of whom all bar Henrietta, the baby of the family, were now dispersed across the length and breadth of the Empire, true sons and daughters of Albion - was greatly troubled with arthritis these days and rarely ventured far from Government House in Philadelphia.

Henrietta, the unfairly regarded as the plainest and rightly judged the brightest of the De L'Isle siblings – in Eleanor's opinion – had largely assumed her mother's role as hostess for official functions and often accompanied her father on his travels acting officially as his personal secretary, and unofficially, as his 'fixer'.

Back in Government House in Philadelphia, where Henrietta worked on the staff of Sir Henry Rawlinson, the Governor's Chief of Staff, De L'Isle's daughter was often referred to as her father's 'road manager'...

The Queen realised she had been wool-gathering.

She met the Governor of New England's eye.

"Seriously, Philip?" She retorted, softening the question by quirking a wan half-smile. Although she was determined to hide it she was still more than a little bit shaken by the events of the afternoon. Like her husband she felt awful about being spirited away when so many people were injured.

The Governor shook his head and sat down.

King George groaned. It had already been a long day and it was not over yet!

There was a knock at the bulkhead door.

"Lady Henrietta has arrived aboard, Your Majesty," an immaculately uniformed Lieutenant reported bowing.

The King shook his head.

Bloody precedence and protocol!

"Wheel her in directly please."

Eleanor was proud of her husband's life-long implacable disinclination to vent his impatience upon a subordinate. His father had been a positive tartar and everybody around him had felt like they were walking on thin ice, or sometimes barefoot on broken glass.

Everybody got to their feet when the Governor's twenty-three-year-old youngest daughter made her entrance.

Henrietta De L'Isle halted briefly and bowed respectfully to the King.

"Your Majesty," she murmured, and: "Ma'am," to Eleanor before hands were being held and pecking kisses on cheeks exchanged. From earliest girlhood the newcomer had only known the King and Queen as her parents' close friends and even now it was very hard for her to think of King George and Queen Eleanor as anything other than Uncle Bertie and Aunt Ellie. The King and Queen both still entertained hopes that their third son, twenty-five-year old James – Prince James, Duke of Cumberland – would do the sensible thing and propose to Henrietta. Problematically, he was having such fun pursuing his career in the Army, with the Blues and Royals, that it was probably far too optimistic to expect him to settle down just yet. And besides, Henrietta had a full-time job in New England at the moment.

"Every time I see you," Eleanor beamed, "you remind me more and more of your dear mother when she was your age, my dear."

"Thank you, Ma'am."

"Your Uncle and Aunt won't hear of cancelling any of tomorrow's engagements, Hen," the young woman's father complained.

"I've had Colonel Harrison of the CSS bending my ear again," Henrietta reported, her tone indicating she was a little dubious about what she had been told. "He says he has evidence of a conspiracy organised by a group called the Sons of Liberty to mount a series of what he calls 'outrages' tomorrow. I asked him if he knew all this why he hadn't done something about it already? He went red in the face and started treating me like a naughty schoolgirl after that." She smiled tight-lipped and glanced to her father. "Sorry about that, Daddy; he'll probably be writing another letter of complaint to you..."

The Governor of New England rolled his eyes.

"The blasted man ought to go through channels like everybody else. These bloody Security Service people cry wolf so often you can't take a thing they say at face value!"

The King was thoughtful.

"Somebody sabotaged the launch of the Polyphemus today, Philip," he remarked sombrely.

A steward entered and began dispensing pre-dinner sherries.

"We didn't know if you were going to be able to join us for dinner, my dear," Eleanor apologised to Henrietta De L'Isle.

The young woman pulled a face, blushed. She tended to make a point of dressing 'as the people dressed' because it gave her a certain anonymity within her father's entourage that enable her to get things done and to 'not be so intimidating'. She was therefore, wearing a stylish but plain blue day dress and her hair was tumbling unrestrained on her shoulders.

"I'm not dressed for..."

"Tom Packenham," the King assured her, "will understand. After today we won't be standing on ceremony at dinner. More to the point your Aunt and I would much rather catch up on your news over dinner than endlessly rehash 'official' business with your misery guts father!"

The Governor chuckled and put his arm around his daughter's shoulders.

"I think that constitutes a royal command, Hen."

In the event it was just Rear Admiral Packenham, his Flag Lieutenant and the four of them in the Squadron Commander's stateroom for dinner.

"We will change tomorrow's schedule," the King decided. That afternoon and evening's engagements had been cancelled pending a reassessment of the security situation. However, tomorrow was Empire Day and he was the bloody King Emperor and nobody was going to tell him what to do in *his* Empire!

He looked to De L'Isle.

"I want to visit the injured in hospital. Can that be accommodated without completely messing up everything else, Philip?"

The Governor of New England thought about this for some moments before turning to his daughter.

The main Empire Day events centred around the Fleet Review and a late afternoon parade at Battery Field. If the weather permitted there was to be a grand reception to be held on the quarterdeck of the Lion for as many as a thousand colonial civil servants and worthies in the evening.

"Most of the injured will have been taken to Queen Mary's Hospital in Brooklyn," Henrietta explained, her brow furrowing, "or to the new Army and Navy Hospital at Flatbush. That's the more modern of the two, I think that's where the most seriously hurt will have been taken. Security wouldn't be such a headache there, either. Daddy's Staff will already be finalising things for tomorrow, if we want to do this we need to get working on it now, sir," she put to the King. "The easiest thing would be to arrange an early morning visit. Literally, at the crack of dawn. Assuming the visit was over and done with by about ten in the morning the rest of the day's events could kick off as planned at eleven o'clock, sir," she reported to the King, her manner that of a practical, very respectful staffer-courtier rather than a favourite honorary niece.

"Philip?" The King asked, looking to his old friend.

The Governor of New England had accepted that his recommendation to drastically cut back, or better still, cancel the Empire Day celebrations had been rejected. Now, it was his job, not to mention the small matter of his duty, simply to 'get on with it'.

"If satisfactory arrangements can be made I have no objection, sir."

"That's settled then. The Queen and I shall visit the Royal Military Hospital at Flatbush first thing in the morning before the Fleet Review," the King declared.

ACT II – EMPIRE DAY

Sunday 4th July 1976

Chapter 17

Brooklyn Admiralty Dockyard, Wallabout Bay, King's County

The *Colonel* had been sitting in John Watson's office when he got back from St Mary's Hospital at one o'clock that morning. Nobody really knew if Matthew Harrison of the Colonial Security Service was actually a colonel, or even how the rank structure of the CSS was organised. Everything about the CSS was smoke and mirrors, myths, rumours, legends. The only thing an honest citizen really needed to know about the CSS was that he, or she, never wanted to have anything to do with it.

By then John Watson was so far beyond the end of his tether that not even finding the most secretive man in New England chain-smoking in his office gave him additional pause for thought.

Three hours after the event he had discovered that his wife had collapsed around the time of the afternoon's disaster and been rushed to hospital with the first badly injured survivors. Something had happened with the baby and by the time she was wheeled into the overwhelmed operating theatres it was too late. An emergency caesarean section had been carried out but the baby – a boy – was already dead and when Watson had finally got to her side Vicky was unconscious, comatose and fighting for her life.

The death toll from the Polyphemus disaster had topped a hundred, with at least as many seriously injured. Some twenty persons were still missing or variously unaccounted for. Among the dead were over forty women and children. Now John Watson's wife was likely dying and he well understood that the only reason 'the Colonel' was sitting in his office was because the CSS was looking for a convenient scapegoat.

"I'm busy, what do you want, Harrison?" He demanded, slumping behind his desk and rifling through the notes which had accumulated on his blotter while he had been at Queen Mary's Hospital. Belatedly, he remembered his manners. A guest was a guest, notwithstanding he was Matthew Harrison. "Forgive me. These are trying hours."

Sixty-two-year old Matthew Jefferson Harrison shrugged.

"No offence taken, friend."

The CSS man had used the time waiting for John Watson's return to study the man's office. His surroundings were less opulent, less to do with a visible expression of his status at the yard, suggesting a confident, pragmatic man who knew he was very good at his job and had no need of the psychological props with which many of his fellows surrounded themselves. The furniture was old, solid and sparse. A big desk, chairs for visitors, a drinks cabinet by the window overlooking the four slipways.

"It has been a long day," Watson breathed wearily. "Will you join me in a drink?"

Presently, Harrison was contemplating the generous measure of Scotch Whiskey in the tumbler in his large, pale hands as the two men took fresh stock of each other, circling like heavyweights nervous about the other man's left hook.

Through the windows arc lights threw their harsh, unrelenting dazzling illumination across a surreal scene as rescuers still sifted through the wreckage at the bottom of the slipway. The hulk of the Polyphemus lay half submerged like a giant steel whale as oxy-acetylene torches cut through the ship's plates in a desperate race to free men still trapped within the hull.

From a distance it might have seemed like an outer ring of Dante's inferno.

"A lot of questions are going to get asked about what happened here today," Harrison observed. "I reckoned I'd start with the man most likely to have figured it out first."

John Watson did not take this as any kind of complement.

"What happened isn't any kind of mystery," he retorted.

Whisky scorched his throat.

Several hundred pounds of most likely blasting powder or gun cotton, cordite – judging by the stench of the remains of the crater half-way down Slipway Number 3 – had detonated during the launch. Thereafter, the forward hull of the Polyphemus had dragged over the wreckage, opening a hundred feet long gash in her bottom plating before she toppled over onto her starboard beam and sank into the relatively shallow waters of Wallabout Bay at the bottom of the slip. The explosion had been so violent it had sent debris as large as slipway rails scything through the packed crowd up to fifty yards away and left a crater over thirty feet wide by ten in depth.

"At some time in the last month saboteurs must have emplaced a large blasting charge in the storm drains beneath the slips..."

"Why the last month?"

Watson emptied his tumbler.

He was an engineer by training so he knew all about the properties of blasting powder and other demolition explosives. Cordite was a low explosive which burned rather than exploded, like TNT, a high explosive. 'Burned' was the operative word. Low explosives only 'exploded' when confined, either in a gun barrel or otherwise. The saboteurs would have had to wall up the storm drain beneath the slipway and that would have blocked it, leading to back flooding if there was a big storm. Without blocking off the tunnel the charge would have burned itself out underground, perhaps venting through weak spots in the drain-lining; and it would not have caused a single violent explosion.

The properties of cordite were so well understood that capital ships like the Lions anchored out in the Upper Bay were designed with 'venting paths' so that flash fires caused by enemy action or by an accident in the shell handling rooms of the main and secondary magazines could never, hopefully, result in a catastrophic ship-wrecking detonation.

"Blocking the storm drains so close to their seaward outfalls would have caused back flooding in Brooklyn and the yards. The last heavy rains were in the first week of June. So, it had to have been done in the last two to three weeks."

"Oh. Right. How big are these drains we're talking about?"

"Four to six feet in diameter. They were installed when the yards were modernised back in the 1950s. The authorities decided it was easier to route them through the yards rather than digging up the neighbourhoods around Brooklyn Heights." He had a stray thought. "Once we dig out the crater and follow the tunnels back we might find traces of the blasting powder or cordite the bastards used. That could be analysed..."

"How do you mean?"

"In peacetime cordite is only made in half-a-dozen factories in the United Kingdom and here in New England. The production process is standardised but there will be minor trace pollutants and imperfections particular to each plant. That would tell us where it came from."

John Watson thought better of it.

"No, that wouldn't help, I suppose."

Under the right conditions gun cotton could be stored for many years, during that time it might be sold on, transferred, or passed through endless hands.

"But," he sighed, "you don't really care about any of that, do you Colonel?"

"Don't I?"

Watson shook his head.

"The CSS didn't see this coming therefore you're doing what everybody else is doing, you're covering your arse!"

"You've got to admit it's mighty suspicious nobody noticed anything was wrong until that bomb went off, friend?"

Watson had walked every inch of Slipway Number 3 in the weeks before the launch, every day checking every little detail, inspecting every block, every chain, every rail. Of course, he had not personally walked and crawled through every drain and utility conduit beneath the slips...

Why would he?

He was damned sure nobody from the Colonial Security Service had either!

John Watson said nothing.

"It doesn't look good," Harrison intoned, clunking down his tumbler half-drunk on the desk.

Chapter 18

East Islip, Suffolk County, Long Island

I honestly did not think this could get more surreal. But then what did I know? The cuffs had come off. I was ordered to take off my wet clothes. A medic had come in and cleaned up my face; and stuffed wads of cotton wool up my nostrils to staunch the flow of blood. Needless to say, nobody brought me dry clothes. Or offered me food or water as I shivered uncontrollably. The thirst was the worst thing, then the cold...

I was beginning to get a feel for 'the method' I was being subjected to. Normally, these things would play out over days; this thing, whatever it was, was operating on a much shorter, possibly abbreviated timescale.

"Drink this."

The water in the beaker tasted brackish but I was so thirsty I'd have drunk the man's piss – anybody's in fact - without a second's hesitation.

Then I got handed a big blanket and led out of my abandoned, coldly tiled abandoned changing room into a cell with a mattress on the floor. This room still retained a little of the sultry heat of the day.

Next, a bowl of some kind of gruel which was vaguely like porridge was put in front of me.

Presently, I began to feel half-human again.

I had just curled up on the mattress and started to nod off to sleep when Sarah marched into the room. One of her acolytes placed a chair for her and she sat, peering down her nose at me.

"When did you discover I was with the CSS?" She asked without preamble.

"When you walked through the door at Long Island University," I confessed. "You were too good to be true."

Sarah raised an eyebrow.

I struggled onto an elbow and eventually sat up, propping my aching frame against the wall at my back.

"I thought you'd play harder to get for longer," I went on. "Don't get me wrong, the sex was good."

This prompted a contemptuous curl of Sarah's lips.

"Well, I enjoyed it, anyway," I assured her in all sincerity.

"Everything's a joke to you, isn't it?"

"We all get by the best we can."

"Tell me about the Sons of Liberty?" This Sarah said crossing her left leg over her right knee in front of my now puffy, possibly blackening eyes. The glimpse of stockinged knee and thigh before her skirt fell back into place allied to my hangover-like headache distracted me so badly I forgot what she had asked me. "The Sons of Liberty?"

"Oh, those old rascals…"

"No, I'm talking about their modern-day co-conspirators?"

I tried to look blank.

"The traitors who use *your* writings as their guiding text!"

"Oh, we're talking about *Two Hundred Lost Years*, again" I muttered. Denying that I was the author of the piece was obviously a waste of time. "You know that was all a joke, don't you? I mean, the sub-title gives the game away. I ask you: *What the World might have looked like if George Washington had ducked at the right time!* Surely, even the CSS ought to get the joke by now?"

Sarah was unblinking.

"The second half of the book," she reminded me tersely, "was an essay about how the World might have looked on the two hundredth anniversary of the treasonous Declaration of Independence on the 4th July 1776 had the rebels wrested the New World out of the hands of Mad King George. You describe England as being a 'tiny little insignificant island off the north-west coast of Europe hankering for its lost world-wide empire..."

I chuckled; I could not help myself.

Sarah glowered at me.

She tried again to refresh my memory: "A tiny little insignificant island off the north-west coast of Europe hankering for its lost world-wide empire forced to beg for scraps off the table of the New Romans governing the globe from their ivory towers in the Americas!"

I did actually recall writing pretty much that.

"You said that George Washington would be remembered as the patriarch of the World's greatest empire and King George III as that 'mad old German loser'!"

"I was writing a satirical polemic. I was a young man and attitudes to these things were, well, different back in the thirties and forties..."

"How do you think King George and Queen Eleanor feel about having their ancestors ridiculed and insulted by people like you?"

"I don't know. Have they actually read any of my books?"

Sarah stood up, rustling in that way that invariably brings warmth to the cockles of an old man's private parts. She moved away, still rustling and stood by the door. The cell was possibly six feet by eight and clearly, she wanted to be a lot farther away from me than that!

I took this as a good omen; I was not about to get slapped again any time soon. Leastways, not by her.

"Look," I said, reasonableness personified or so I thought, "a lot of contemporary historians, here and in England, see the crushing of the rebellion in 1776 as a pivotal point in imperial history. Without the resources of New England at its disposal the British might have had to fight a world war on two fronts – with the rebel colonies at their backs - when the French wars of the 1790s flared up. And later, when the German Empire was at its most aggressively expansionary how could Britain have matched it industrially, or militarily without the factories and manpower of New England. Goodness, had the colonies gained their freedom in the 1770s they might have allied with France and Spain against England at any time in the late eighteenth and throughout most of the nineteenth century. So, absolutely, if the Continental Army had not been destroyed in August 1776 and the one man capable of leading its surviving remnants had not been killed at the battle of Long Island, the World in which we are living today might indeed be a radically different, and perhaps, a better place to live. It is all academic, anyway, just an intriguing thought exercise."

"Don't you teach your students that 'the tongue is mightier than the blade'?"

Actually, I usually misquoted dear old Euripides – who died around 400 BC, so far as I recollected, so, he would not mind – by opining that 'the pen is mightier than the sword'.

"Yes, but that was in the context of the Bible, the Koran or the wisdom of the ancient Greeks, or Confucius, not my own humble scribblings, my dear."

"Nonetheless your followers call you the Father of Liberty?"

"My followers?"

"You started by poisoning your sons' minds against the Crown then you sowed sedition..."

I thought I was the one who had been drugged!

"I've done no such thing!"

That was when a very strange thing happened; possibly the strangest thing yet. Sarah started crying.

I struggled to my feet, would have crumpled to the floor had I not braced myself against the wall for a moment.

"Don't touch me!"

I had not planned on touching her. I was a sucker for tears, that's all. I held up my hands.

"How could you do it?" Sarah spat at me.

"Do what?" I asked like an idiot, completely blindsided.

"Blow up that ship and kill all those people?"

I opened my mouth to ask the obvious question.

"What," I stuttered. "What are you talking about?"

"Don't you dare pretend you don't know exactly what I'm talking about. You're a monster!" Sarah shuddered with sudden, unmistakable revulsion. "I can't believe I let you *touch* me!"

It was a bit late to be crying foul.

However, I refrained from voicing this sentiment.

"You have to give me the names of the people responsible. Now! Or I won't answer for what will happen to Alex and Abe," she took a snarling gulp of air, and added, posthumously: "and Bill!"

"They've done nothing," I protested, hoarsely. "None of us have and you know it!"

We were shouting at each other like an old married couple who had hated each other all along.

"I know that you are the leader of the Sons of Liberty..."

"That's horse manure!"

"Names! I want names, Isaac!"

Sarah and I were toe to toe, breathless with anger.

"For once in your miserable life do the decent thing, man!"

Chapter 19

Jamaica Bay Field, King's County, Long Island

Alex Fielding had invited his two 'wingmen' to join him sampling the delights of nearby St Albans. He had considered – albeit in passing – looking up his father in Gravesend; but decided against it. Dad got preachy every year around the time of the Empire Day holidays and they would almost certainly get into a fight about his shameless 'profiteering' flying press men and photographers over the Fleet Review.

So, St Albans it had been!

Neither Paul Hopkins or Rufus McIntyre had wanted to join him on his expedition back to the less than exotic fleshpots of his misspent youth. This was a thing he breathed a heartfelt sigh of relief over as soon as he was a safe distance away from the pair of them.

Neither of the idiots was half the pilot Abe was and Abe was just starting out; it had been all the losers could do to keep formation with him in straight and level flight. He had lost them in an instant the moment he started 'beating up' Leppe Island; later Hopkins had got lost following him down to Long Island and he had had to turn around and reel him back in!

Never mind, they had both touched down – more or less – safely on the grassy strip overlooking the marshy wetlands the first settlers had called Jamaica Bay, so called probably, as Dad would say 'because they were so badly lost they had no idea if they were in Jamaica or Boston!'

Anyway, Alex had met a girl called Daisy who had cleaned him out every which way, had a good time and hitched a ride back to the field in the early hours of the morning and slept the sleep of the just.

"Are you Alexander Fielding?" The bespectacled man in

the plus fours asked hesitantly.

Alex groaned and blinked up at the stranger.

"Yeah, who would you be, sir?"

"Albert Stanton of the Manhattan Globe," the other man confessed. "Are you drunk?"

"Nope," Alex declared, shaking his head and rising unsteadily to his feet. "But I will be again later. We agreed thirty-five pounds, Mr Stanton?"

"Er, yes..."

"I'll take you as low and as close to the big ships as I'm allowed but if we get too close they might open fire on us." Alex had been trying to be funny; the other man gave him a cold fish look. "What?" He asked.

"After what happened at the Brooklyn Navy Yard yesterday I should imagine the Navy is as trigger happy as Hell!"

Alex ran a hand through his tousled hair.

His bladder was fit to burst.

"Excuse me," he turned away and after fumbling with his flies relieved himself on the ground beneath his Bristol V.

He saw the line of Jerry cans nearby. *Excellent!* The gasoline he had paid for last night prior to his sortie to St Albans – while he still had money in his pockets - had materialised overnight. He buttoned his trousers. "That's better! Give me a hand with those cans and we'll be on our way!"

For some minutes the strenuous work of pouring 87-octane fuel into the old trainer's tank passed wordlessly.

"What happened at Brooklyn yesterday?" Alex inquired belatedly. More to be civil than from any existential curiosity.

"There was a dreadful accident, some say sabotage, at the launch of HMS Polyphemus. Over a hundred people were killed and the CSS have been making large scale arrests.

"Oh, maybe I won't fly as close as I usually do to Navy ships today!"

From the look on Albert Stanton's face the photographer suspected he was about to be short-changed. The first aircraft were running up their engines.

Alex checked the field's windsock and flags.

The wind was southerly to south westerly.

A little high cloud apart the sky was already azure blue all the way to the invisible stars above.

Stanton had one of the new heavyweight British cameras with a stubby telescopic lens. Seeing Alex's interest in his equipment the man in spectacles became positively loquacious.

"I'm using the latest Ealing one-inch colour stock film today. So, especially as the sun is quite low at this time of day I need to be 'down sun' to avoid extraneous glare off the water..."

"Do you need to land to re-load a new magazine of film?"

"No, that's the marvellous thing about these cameras."

"Do you want to go in the front or the back seat? This is a dual control machine so it doesn't matter to me."

Passengers usually wanted to go in the front seat but Stanton was a professional and he knew he would get better shots, less obstructed by the wings from the back seat.

Out of the corner of his eye Alex saw Rufus McIntyre and Paul Hopkins trudging towards their Bristol VIs like men off to the funeral of somebody they despised. They had had their aircraft fuelled up last night. Alex had been unwilling to pay a premium for the privilege, not everybody was made of money.

Alex gave Albert Stanton the normal 'talk' as the two of them went to the tail of the Bristol, picked it up and walked it around until the nose of the trainer was pointing into the wind.

"Make sure you are strapped in at all times"

"Hang onto your camera like grim death."

"Don't touch any of the controls."

And: "Don't be sick until we're back on the ground again!"

Then Alex was running up the engine.

Chapter 20

Leppe Island, Montgomery County, New York

Abe Fielding had been aware from a relatively young age that in its tribal grounds the Iroquois Nation operated so separately from the normal colonial administration that it, in effect, constituted a kind of shadow, or ghost society. It was more than just separate development, it was a nation within a nation in the northern counties of New York. However, it was only when in late adolescence that he realised that 'the system' might have been designed to stop Kate and he being together the way his own father and mother had been that he had really understood both its cruel iniquities and the remarkable possibilities it might offer a self-elected fugitive.

In the 'white' colonies of the East Coast a man needed identification papers to prove ownership, and as an adult a web of contracts determined his place in that society; among the tribes of the Iroquois peoples there were no records, no formal checks or balances other than personal recommendation, or a friend or an ally or a kinsman to vouch for one, no meaningful money economy, everything was personal, not commercial and every social transaction was by the free will of all the parties concerned.

Obviously, the system was imperfect and human foibles and follies made for what in Abe's world might have been called a feudal society but that said, there were few native tricksters and shysters preying on the unwary and the vulnerable, violence was restricted in the main to consenting males, and more often than not expressed in ritualised non-lethal forms and unquestionably, the biggest difference from the 'white' colonial model, was that women were regarded as equal members of most communities.

In other words, the worst excesses of *Getrennte*

Entwicklung in the First Thirteen colonies – directed against blacks in the south and mainly against the native nations of the north – had created not just 'separate' communities but an underground movement of which the Colonial authorities knew little and understood less. Since most whites did not consider full-blood Indians or African-Americans as citizens, and in some places did not regard or treat persons so classified even as human beings the borders of tribal lands and former slave reservations were porous, unregulated. The situation skewed trade and consequently the tax-raising competence of individual colonies creating huge unregulated, shadowy black-market sectors in every local economy and meant that it was hard if not impossible to track people or realistically, to control cross-border movements.

The really odd thing was that most white colonists – certainly most of their leaders – either did not see the problem or simply did not understand the way clinging to, and latterly, actively pursuing *Getrennte Entwicklung* policies had hollowed out the eastern half of New England. Society and the economy had stagnated in the East while in the Mississippi valley and many of the western colonies and territories, despite the never-ending Border War in the South West, migration from the old 'First Thirteen' colonies had fuelled a twenty-year runaway boom. Out west there was still unclaimed land and new industries had sprung up along the whole length of the mighty Mississippi from the Canadian border to the Gulf of Spain twelve hundred miles to the south. Out in the 'new colonies' there was little of the bureaucracy that strangled daily life and business on the East Coast, no straightjacket of stupid 'Separate Development' legislation and the hand of imperial administration was 'light' to 'non-existent'. The West was once what the East had been a hundred years ago, the great unstoppable economic and commercial engine of the North

American continent allowed to run free by the masters of the colonies back in London.

What so many religious fundamentalists in the East viewed as a slow disintegration of moral and religious coherence was really just the logical corollary to the unresolved imbroglio of the border with the Empire of Nuevo España, and the hiving off of between twenty and thirty percent of all the land of their own colonies into huge ghettos or tribal lands where the white man's writ no longer ran, and the ever-quickening pace of change in the far west.

Abe had no illusion that as he and Kate packed up their camp early that morning that he was about to become anything other than a fugitive voluntarily exiled from the society into which he had been born; and that among his own people in the twin-colony there would be little or no Christian sympathy for his decision.

To the *Getrennte Entwicklung* crowd, he was a moral and racial degenerate 'going native'; to the authorities he would be a runaway shirking his responsibilities to his Colony, a draft-dodging good for nothing who had cheated the Commonwealth of New York-Long Island of his period of medical indenture. If he ever returned he might be arrested and if he failed to recant and to fulfil his servitude to the Colony, face imprisonment. The shame would live with him forever.

Kate was subdued.

"I know what it is that you do for me," she said eventually as they carried their bags through the trees to where they had hidden the two canoes. Invisibly through the foliage they heard her father and cousins breaking camp; the group would travel together deeper into the Iroquois Nation before the husband and wife finally went their own way. "I know what you are giving away."

Abe halted, put down his load and turned to face Kate.

"I am giving away nothing that is of any worth in the

world and gaining everything that is," he shrugged, "priceless, *Rone.*"

She threw her arms around his neck and he wrapped her in a bear hug that lifted her feet off the ground as they kissed.

"Tekonwenaharake," he whispered in her ear, "she whose voice travels through the wind," he cooed, "without you I am like dust in that wind."

Kate sniffed, kissed him again.

Stepped back, and with a giggle, frowned.

"Men are so full of shit!" She murmured in Kanien'keháka, with a limpid-eyed fondness.

"This is true," he confessed.

Chapter 21

HMS Cassandra, Upper Bay, New York

The sleek fleet destroyer had come alongside HMS Lion during the night. The King, the Queen and their entourage had gone onboard while it was still dark and stepped off the Cassandra onto Gravesend Pier literally at the crack of dawn for the short drive – about four miles – inland to the Royal Military Hospital located on the outskirts of the town of Flatbush. The Lieutenant Governor of Long Island had sent his Rolls-Royce to collect the King and Queen, and other members of the party were accommodated in one or other of the dozen or so Land Rovers and cars waiting 'in convoy', which was to be led and trailed by armoured cars of the 16th Lancers.

To assert that security for this hastily scheduled 'visit' was 'heavy' would be to recklessly understate the case. The road from the coast to Flatbush had been cleared with military vehicles blocking every side turn, and infantrymen in full battle order patrolling everywhere. Belying this visible demonstration of armed might the hospital itself had had less than an hour's notice of the visitation, and other than lending his official car, the Lord Lieutenant had been asked to not alter his personal Empire Day diary so as to avoid drawing too much attention to Flatbush ahead of the King and Queen's arrival.

King George was hugely impressed, as he invariably was, by the efficiency with which his own Household, his advisors, colonial administrators and the armed services facilitated, and obediently carried out his commands.

If only we ran the rest of the Empire the same way...

In his unscheduled absence from the flagship the Governor of the Commonwealth of New England had been left 'holding the fort' and acting as the King's Chief of Staff.

Something always came up at the worst possible moment in the run up to great state ceremonial demonstrations and whatever came up the King implicitly trusted Philip De L'Isle to 'sort it out'.

The visit to the hospital had been harrowing. These things often were in his experience. Without Eleanor he would have been lost, a useless stuffed shirt in a ridiculous antique uniform!

The old fuddy-duddies in his father's court still tut-tutted but trying to stop Eleanor hugging a sick child or comforting a grieving mother, father, daughter, brother or sister was like Canute trying to hold back the tide.

The Queen simply was not made that way.

George was proud of her. Of course, he was always proud of her but that morning, especially so after the trauma of yesterday. Because she was so naturally tactile it suddenly became a hundred times easier for him to forget that he was the King Emperor and behave like a normal human being. The old King had never picked up a child in his life; not even one of his own. The very thought would have horrified the old curmudgeon and given half his doddering old courtiers a nervous breakdown!

As for King George's mother. Goodness, once she had squeezed out sufficient 'spares' to preserve the royal line she had washed her hands of her offspring until they were toileted, well-mannered, presentable in public and more or less educated.

Tactile had been a swear word in the Royal palaces of England for a generation until Eleanor had come upon the scene, first as HRH, the Duchess of Windsor in a small way, and then as Queen Consort, in a way that had made her the nation's and the Empire's Queen Mother almost overnight.

The King had taken the son of a maimed dockyard worker in his arms, Eleanor had embraced the boy's mother, sat awhile with her holding her hand.

How on earth could people be so solicitous about us at such a dreadful time?

There were still people in England, within the Royal Household, the establishment and the Government, who disapproved of his and Eleanor's 'way of monarchy'. The diehards still imagined that in this modern, technological age when the globe was connected by radio and television, in which the gathering cry for self-determination and a loosening of the shackles of empires was daily shaping social and political changes unimagined only twenty years ago, that the Monarchy could somehow remain the unchanging, rigid monolith that it had been for centuries.

An enormous crowd had gathered on Gravesend Pier by the time the Royal Party returned to board the Cassandra.

"Don't let go of my hand, my dear," Eleanor murmured as they stepped out of the Rolls-Royce. She had dried up her tears on the short ride from the hospital. "I must look red-eyed and blotchy," she sighed.

"Not a bit of it, my love!"

They went straight to the barrier where behind a line of infantrymen – regulars not militiamen – a throng of cheering men, women and children had awaited, patiently for a glimpse of the royal couple, possibly for many hours.

"Why, thank you for coming out to see us," Eleanor beamed at the sea of faces.

The King doffed his cap to the crowd.

Henrietta De L'Isle had scurried across the pier, heedless of her own dignity, and virtually on hands and knees planted a single microphone on a stand before the King and Queen.

Goodness, Eleanor thought, *that girl thinks of everything!*

"The Queen and I," the King declared, "have had the honour of visiting a number of the men, women and children so grievously injured in yesterday's outrage in Brooklyn, and sadly, the opportunity to give what little comfort we might to those whose loved ones have perished, or for whom there must be little hope of recovery. As always, we were humbled by the fortitude, courage and pluck of everybody we encountered."

At a squeeze of his hand he surrendered the microphone to his wife.

"We cannot praise the tireless work of the dedicated doctors and nurses at the Flatbush Royal Military Hospital enough. Tragically, it is only at the worst of times that one becomes aware of the very best in us all. I could not help but weep, neither of us could, meeting so many good people laid low through no fault of their own, and yet so bravely confronting things..."

Eleanor's voice failed her. She lowered her head for a moment, sniffed back a flood of tears. Overhead two aircraft circled like distracting, angrily buzzing bees as she re-composed herself.

"It is at times like this, on days like this that I and my husband are reminded that we are honoured and privileged to be *your* King and Queen, and we are reminded that the only reason that *we* are here today is to serve *you!*"

The King drew his wife's hand to his side and she moved close.

Spontaneously, he planted a pecking kiss on her cheek, and in a similar moment of abandon she kissed him back.

"God save you all!" King George declared.

The Royal Standard broke from the port halyard of the destroyer's old-fashioned mainmast.

Onboard HMS Cassandra as the warship cast off and began to back away from the pier the King and Queen waved to the masses.

"I'm sorry, I didn't mean to get so emotional," Eleanor said, smiling despite her roiling angst.

"You are *their* Queen, my love," her husband reassured her. "You are their Queen and the Mother of the Empire. The world is changing and there are no rules in the King and

Queen game anymore."

She leaned against him as they smiled their fixedly regal smiles.

Henrietta De L'Isle and her two personal bodyguards had literally jumped onto the destroyer as she departed. Now the young woman approached her Sovereign.

She was a little breathless. "I'm sorry, I should have had that microphone in place before your car arrived, sir."

The King laughed. "My dear, you are a marvel!"

"Oh," Henrietta blushed and momentarily stared at her feet. "I, well... Thank you, sir..."

The King waved one last time and turned away from the pier, now some fifty to sixty yards away.

"We shall repair to the wardroom," he commanded. "My wife and I need a stiff drink before we show our faces again!"

The original schedule for this day, Empire Day, had ordained that the King and Queen should attend morning service on the quarterdeck of the Lion, and partake of sherry and sweetmeats in the flagship's wardroom preparatory to boarding the Cassandra shortly before eleven o'clock.

Thereupon, the Fleet Review would commence with the destroyer steaming slowly up and down the columns of ships anchored in the Lower and Upper Bays for well over two hours amidst the constant firing of royal salutes, the flying of thousands of flags, and the cheering of every ship's company as it lined the rail.

These things almost always over ran; for one, both bays would be full of sailing craft and motor boats impeding Cassandra's stately progress; and for two, it was a huge party and nobody worried overmuch if a party went on a little longer than the timespan mentioned on the original invitation!

Henrietta De L'Isle and the Queen disappeared briefly while the King chatted with the destroyer's second-in-command – the Captain was making sure Cassandra did not run down any of the yachts cluttering Gravesend Bay – and Eleanor re-emerged with her face 'restored'.

Word came from the bridge that 'Cassandra will be on station in ten minutes', and the Royal Party dutifully trekked up to the destroyer's open compass platform.

Cassandra's modern successors had enclosed bridges; marvellous for conning the ship in a North Atlantic blow but not so good for viewing and being viewed during the course of a Fleet Review.

The destroyer was making fifteen knots through the slight chop in the Lower Bay, hurrying to her start position abreast the starboard flank of HMS Lion by the appointed hour. The ship cleft through the sea with effortless ease, the roar of her engine room blowers like the purring of a mighty beast of prey.

Eleanor put a hand to her head, wondering if perhaps she ought to put her hat back on before her hair became totally windswept.

Soon Cassandra would sweep through the narrows – Hell's Gate - into the Upper Bay, still rushing until she came abreast of the Tiger, the fourth ship in the 5th Battle Squadron 'line'.

Each of the Lions had supposedly been built to the same 'class pattern' but a professional eye could pick out a myriad of minor distinguishing differences between the great ships; service refits, retrofits and upgrades to their upper works, masts, ELDAR aerials and arrays, and communications antenna which readily identified each as being unique.

For example, third in the line was the Queen Elizabeth, the least modified of the four ships still operating with her original ELDAR rig and twenty-year-old main battery gun directors. Of course, to a casual observer, or at a distance all of the Lions seemed identical, virtually indistinguishable from the smaller heavy cruisers Ajax and Naiad flanking the flagship.

All the visiting Navies had been allocated anchorages in the Lower Bay either side of the ships of the 3rd and 5th Cruiser Squadrons, the nucleus of the Americas-stationed East Coast Fleet. Presently, the flagship of the ECF, the massive battlecruiser Indomitable, was dry-docked at Norfolk having been in collision with a merchantman in Chesapeake Bay a month ago. Nevertheless, her two sisters, the thirty-year old Invincible and Indefatigable swung around their chains in the middle of the Lower Bay dwarfing practically every other ship bar the visitors from Kiel.

The German Empire had sent the 2nd Battle Squadron of the High Seas Fleet across the Atlantic with a bevy of escorting destroyers. Just to remind the Royal Navy that if it neglected the Home Fleet the North Sea and the Atlantic sea lanes might not be forever the British 'ponds' they had been for most of the last two hundred years.

The Imperial German Navy, numerically and technically second only to the Royal Navy – upon which it modelled its organisation, training, operational practices and traditions – had sent three of its most formidable capital ships to New England.

The Kaiser Wilhelm, and her sisters the Grosser Kurfurst and Friedrich der Grosse were fifty-thousand-ton leviathans with main batteries and systems of armoured protection mirroring that of the Lion and the subsequent Victory class battleships currently serving with the Home Fleet. Many naval architects regarded the Kaiser Wilhelm class as improved 'copies' of the Lions, and possibly superior and more robust gun platforms, given that the first of them had only been laid down some years after the Lion had been commissioned. The Germans had always refuted any suggestion that they had 'copied' the design of the Lions, rightly pointing out that the Kaiser Wilhelms had adopted a significantly different hull form.

They were almost as long as the Lions but seven or eight

feet broader in the beam, with their main armoured deck – protected by a 6-inch shell of Krupp cemented steel - positioned seven feet lower in that wider hull, a thing made necessary because their machinery was supposedly more modern, and therefore lighter than that of the Lions, necessitating the redistribution of weight lower in the hull to thus maintain the optimum metacentric height (GM) – the distance between a ship's centre of gravity and its centre of buoyancy – to ensure that the ship remained a stable gun platform.

German naval architects tended to aim for a slightly higher GM number – as many as two to three feet higher – than their British counterparts. For the Kaiser Wilhelms the number was between nine and ten feet; for the Lions around six to seven feet when they were fully loaded. This meant that the German ships were stiffer; faster in the roll and less comfortable sea boats in heavy weather, and the British slower to swing back through the horizontal making them intrinsically better gun platforms in any kind of seaway.

In terms of gunnery speed of roll had been the crucial thing throughout most of history, certainly since the first cannon went to sea. Nowadays, it was less so, with gyroscopic gun directors capable of identifying the exact moment the ship was level regardless of the speed of the roll, and electrical fire circuits synchronising salvos and broadsides with that critical 'moment'.

The King was old-school about these things.

The Kaiser Wilhelms were built to fight in the North Sea or the Baltic, *His* ships were built to fight in any ocean anywhere in the World in any conditions.

The King mulled this and other questions as he studied the three German monsters moored to starboard of the immensely more ascetically pleasing, if less durable silhouettes of the two Formidable class battlecruisers. The Formidables, with their thin deck armour would be no match for the Kaiser Wilhelms in a stand-up fight despite the fact that they carried comparable main batteries.

The battlecruisers belonged to a bygone age.

He guessed that any of the Lions would be a match for the newer German pretenders. He did not understand why the Imperial Navy had allowed its architects to put that armoured deck so low in their ships. What use was an unsinkable steel raft if most of the men in the ship were on top of it?

It was all academic; the British and German Empires were allies, after all...

Cassandra's signalling lamp was clattering noisily – the device was a modified searchlight with shutters that banged open and shut with metallic insouciance as messages were exchanged – on the port bridge wing.

The King had briefly been lost in his thoughts.

He blinked back to the here and the now.

"Sorry, my dear," he apologised, realising belatedly that his wife had spoken to him

"Was that an explosion, Bertie?" She asked with barely contained alarm.

The King – who had been a gunnery specialist in his early naval career and was therefore a little deafer than he ought to be for a man still only in his late middle years - had been staring at the forward main battery gun director position of the Grosser Kurfurst.

He followed his wife's gaze, past the looming bulk of the Invincible and the Indefatigable towards the narrows where he could just make out the Tiger, the rearmost Lion of the 5th Battle Squadron.

He blinked in disbelief.

There was a crimson flash and a roiling mushroom of grey-black smoke.

And then, distantly, another.

Chapter 22

Jamaica Bay Field, King's County, Long Island

Alex Fielding had had a good morning. After he got back from taking Albert Stanton over the fleet he had taken to the air with one of the Manhattan Globe man's competitors and now he had nearly a hundred pounds sterling in his pocket! The last dope had paid him a twenty pounds bonus for taking a detour north over Wallabout Bay so he could snap a few pictures of the Polyphemus lying on her side. From all the activity on the half-submerged hull it seemed likely that they were still trying to get people out of the sunken ship. Just the thought of being trapped in the darkness with the water rising around him gave him nightmares.

He hated confined spaces...

Anyway, somebody else's misfortune was usually somebody's opportunity and so it had proved for him. As if he had not already had a good morning when he looked up from refuelling his trusty Bristol V it was to see his next ride getting out of her car. She was almost on time, too. No problem, he had had to go under the cowling to monkey about with the plugs anyway when he had landed.

"I'm the Honourable Leonora Coolidge, Mister Fielding," the woman announced.

Even if she had not been smoking a cigarette and Alex had not just splashed a pint of 87-octane gasoline down his pants she would have been the sort of woman who made him nervous.

She had turned up in a chauffeur-driven Bentley and she was dressed in the sort of flying leathers and boots only very rich people and strippers wear in public.

Alex took an involuntary step backwards.

"I'd shake your hand but you want to put that smoke out

first," he explained hurriedly, "or we'll both go up in flames."

The woman gave him a thoughtful look, then, smelling the petrol vapour in the air, she worked it out for herself.

She took a step back and ground out the cigarette beneath her heel.

"Forgive me. I don't usually fly in such small aeroplanes," she informed the pilot.

"Sorry about the way I look. I've been up a couple of times already this morning and had to do some work on the engine just now," he blurted, still a little intimidated by Leonora Coolidge.

She was blond – from what he could see of the hair sticking out of her brown leather flying skull-cap – and willowy, late twenties maybe and her eyes were very nearly cornflower blue.

"Oh," Alex added, "and you always get gasoline on you when you refuel these kites on your own."

The woman contemplated the whiplash fit tousled haired man in the oil-stained flying suit, sizing him up. She guessed he was a little older than her, and his face was weathered, had about it a prize-fighter's propensity to take hard knocks if that was what it took to get the job done.

That said she remained unimpressed by his aeroplane.

It looked like it was made of coarse canvas and held together by cane and cat gut.

The man was reading her thoughts.

"Don't get carried away by the way she looks," he chuckled. "This old bird's a lot tougher than you or me!"

Leonora Coolidge's driver was standing by his vehicle, ready to open the door so that his ride could get back in.

"Your guy got a name?" Alex inquired, nodding at the man.

"Joe."

"Once you're in the front seat I'll need him to give me a hand pointing the aircraft into the wind."

"You're ready to go?"

"Sure. When you are."

That made up her mind.

Her fiancé had offered to fly her over the review in his De Havilland twin-engined racer – a gilded carriage in comparison with the heap of scrap in front of her now – but they had had a tiff and she had decided that she was going to fly over the Fleet with or without the assistance of that no-good piece of...

Leonora climbed into the machine with no little trepidation.

A single slip and she strongly suspected that she would put her foot through the fuselage and probably fall to the ground!

She was a little irked to be treated like a child.

"Make sure you are strapped in at all times"

"Don't touch any of the controls in the front cockpit."

And: "Don't be sick until we're back on the ground again!"

Then Alex was running up the engine and waving at Leonora's driver, Joe, to pick up the tail and walk it around to the north.

Leonora heard and felt the engine quieten.

Nothing happened.

"What are we waiting for?" She shouted.

Alex had been watching Rufus McIntyre's Bristol VI waddle across the turf like a baby elephant trying to get airborne by flapping its ears. It eventually got off the ground just short of the sandy marshland bordering the eastern side of the field.

He pointed sidelong at Paul Hopkins's aircraft repeating McIntyre's slow-motion, horribly laboured take-off run.

The two idiots had been sitting around all morning while everybody else had been flying their socks off and now both men were taking off slightly across the wind.

"I'm waiting to see if that fellow crashes or not!"

The second Bristol VI took an even longer run up before staggering into the air at the very last moment.

What on earth do those comedians think they are doing taking-off in aircraft so obviously over-loaded?

Sooner or later the authorities were going to have to do something to stop every Tom, Dick or Harry – or Rufus or Paul – going flying. Those two would not be the only complete beginners, regardless of what their pilot's logs said they were, in Alex's humble opinion, rank amateurs, taking to the sky as they pleased today.

Not my problem, thank goodness!

He gunned the motor and the trainer lurched forward.

Soon she was bumping, running across the grass.

Opening up the throttle the engine bellowed and the old biplane lifted effortlessly, as light as a feather off the turf and began to climb over Rockaway Point, the long sandy isthmus that sheltered Gravesend and Jamaica bays from the winter storms.

The aircraft soared high above a destroyer slowly quartering the entrance to the Lower Bay between Rockaway Point in the north and Sandy Hook to the south.

The whole Lower Bay in the west seemed full of column after column of grey warships streaming a thousand flags and pennants in the brilliant morning sunshine.

Leonora had only ever flown in the relative luxury of a passenger cabin of a big two or four propeller air-liner or Imperial Airways flying boat – aerial gin palaces by any other name – or in one or other of her beau's, there had been three or four in the last couple of years, shiny, super-fast racers or airborne playthings. The men she became 'involved with' all had aeroplanes or noisy, over-powered motor launches, souped-up over-powered speedboats by any other name, like the ones ripping up the waves far down below.

She twisted in her seat.

"CAN WE GO LOWER?"

The man grinned and nodded, gave her a thumb's up signal and the old aircraft dove towards the ships in the mile-wide narrows between Long Island and Staten Island.

They flew over the top of a huge battleship, so low that Leonora imagined she could smell the fumes coming out of the ship's after smoke stack.

Then they were climbing, soaring over the next leviathan.

There was an orange-red flicker of light below her.

Suddenly the aircraft was on its side.

Leonora felt the hot blast of air on her face and the machine tip over and start to fall out of the air.

Somebody screamed in feral, animal terror.

It was a second or two before she realised that she was the one who was screaming.

Chapter 23

HMS Lion, Upper Bay, New York

Rear Admiral Sir Thomas Pakenham eyed the aircraft circling over the fleet and the chaotic proliferation of motor boats and yachts of practically every conceivable size and rig milling in between the big ships with a very jaundiced eye. Fleet Reviews were staid, disciplined affairs in home waters but out in the colonies they were always circuses. Given what had happened yesterday afternoon he had quietly, very strongly advised the King that either there should be a general prohibition on small craft or the whole thing should be called off. His old friend had politely and very firmly rebuffed his advice.

It was Empire Day and 'a lot of people will have been looking forward to this day for a long time'.

Including, the commander of the 5th Battle Squadron reflected, a lot of people with malice aforethought!

Problematically, as the Review was to be held in the waters of the Crown Colonies of New York-Long Island *and* New Jersey the whole thing had had to be organised by the combine 'Fleet Review Committees' of both colonies; the members of which spent the rest of their lives in cut-throat competition, and basically, really did not like each other. Wisely, the Governor of New England had tried to keep above the fray, acting as an impartial referee employing his most diplomatic staffers as peace-making go-betweens as the arrangements had finally been agreed, line by painful line over the course of the last six months.

Allegedly, the Fleet Review Committee had disintegrated into open warfare – albeit nothing more unpleasant than ineffectual fisticuffs – several times over the last few weeks and only the intercession of the Governor's daughter, Henrietta, shuttling between the alienated factions had avoided her father having to opt for the so-called 'Flanders Option', so named after a particularly bloody Allied victory in France in 1864, removing the whole thing from the hands of the 'local' colonies. No Governor in living memory had wanted to do that about anything, let alone an event designed to be an Imperial celebration of everybody's loyalty to the Crown!

Young Henrietta was a marvel!

Even after she had knocked the warring parties' heads together she remained, apparently, the most sought-after guest at any reception held in either New Jersey or New York-Long Island in the coming social season when all the great families of the First Thirteen 'brought out' their daughters.

Nevertheless, the soul of the Commander of the 5th Battle Squadron was restless. The King and Queen's mission ashore in Flatbush that morning had further troubled Pakenham as he paced the lofty flying bridge atop his flagship's broad citadel-like forward superstructure. In action he would retreat to the compass platform a deck below; up here in the open air the concussion of the forward 15-inch guns could easily knock a man off his feet or concuss him insensible or worse.

HMS Lion's captain was no less anxious.

"We knew it was going to be chaos but this is ridiculous, sir," he observed to Packenham as the two men eyed the countless small boats criss-crossing the Upper Bay. It was a miracle that there was not a collision a minute!

"Ours' is not to reason why," the Squadron Commander guffawed as if he had not a worry in the world. Nonetheless, he had ordered all the Royal Navy ships moored in the Upper Bay to observe maximum watertight integrity – that is, to dog shut all bulkheads below the waterline and to exclude sea duty men from 'parade duties dressing ship'. Just in case anything amiss did occur he wanted at least half the guns manned, and all damage control and emergency teams ready, waiting and in position. Moreover, he had ordered that all four Lions 'light off' at least a pair of boilers in their second fire rooms.

Each battleship had four boiler rooms – or fire rooms as they were increasingly termed these days – and four turbine compartments, with a boiler room-turbine room 'set' each turning one of the battleships' screws.

Fear nothing but be ready for anything!

"Cassandra is signalling, sir!"

The Squadron Commander glanced to the binnacle clock.

Ten-fifty-seven-hours; the King was going to arrive just in time!

Tom Packenham regarded this as a minor miracle and hoped it boded well for the rest of the day.

One of the big, super-charged speed boats so in vogue in the East Coast colonies roared close down the Lion's flank with its two in-line customised aero-engines purring malevolently. The boat left a turbulent wake lapping ineffectually at the waterlines of the four Lions, castles of steel not to be undermined by the passing of a relative minnow no matter how fast or how loud it was.

The finest racing yachts had been built in New England for a century, lately the colonists' obsession for speed had found expression in the competition to continually edge up the world land, water and airspeed records, all of which were now held by New Englanders or industrial conglomerates based in the Americas.

"All ships will signal non-authorised vessels to keep a safe distance from Cassandra!"

The trouble with civilians on the water was that they paid absolutely no attention to signals, or orders of any kind unless or until one put a shot across their bows!

At that very minute Cassandra's captain would be pouring on the revolutions to ensure that the King was not late for his own party. The destroyer was still too far away, her low silhouette still blurred in the haze but Packenham imagined her creaming through the narrows with a rare bone in her teeth.

The Squadron Commander forced himself to relax as he stepped to the front of the flying bridge to take in the vista of New York City occupying the bottom two to three square miles of Manhattan Island and the broad, orderly streets ascending Brooklyn Heights on the western shore of Long Island.

Yesterday's disaster at Wallabout Bay left a foul taste in his mouth, not least because the Colonial Security Service had – peremptorily, with somewhat ill-grace he felt - turned down his offer to send members of his staff and the Squadron Engineering Division to assist in surveying the damage to the facilities on land and the condition of the wreck of HMS Polyphemus.

Once the Fleet Review was done and dusted the men of the 5th Battle Squadron were looking forward to a well-earned run ashore. Not in the staid, well-policed city on the southern tip of Manhattan but farther up the East River in the flesh pots of New Town where every sailor who had ever visited New York seemed to end up. All big ports had their drinking, whoring more or less anything goes red-light districts and since time immemorial New Town had been New York's...

"My God!" The Lion's Captain gasped in horror.

Packenham wheeled around and strode to join the men leaning over the starboard bridge rail peering astern.

"Something's just blown up alongside the Princess Royal!"

HMS Lion's Captain did not wait for his Admiral's order.

"SOUND THE BELL FOR ACTION STATIONS!"

Chapter 24

Upper Bay, New York

Alex Fielding did not know what had just happened but *knowing* was secondary, understanding at an intuitive, visceral level was *everything*, the difference between life and death. When something blew up close to a string-bag like a Bristol V the world went to Hell in a hurry and the only thing that mattered was stopping the kite nose-diving into the earth or the water. He had yanked the stick to the left, kicked the rudder bar and gunned the engine before he consciously registered what he was doing.

The old trainer was still inverted.

He hoped Leonora Coolidge had strapped herself in as tightly as he had told her to; a woman like that was not to be wasted.

He was hanging on his straps.

The Bristol V wanted to spin; he knew that if she did that at this low level he was a dead man.

Still upside down the aircraft careened insanely between the tall grey smoke stacks of one of the Lions so close that it was probably the updraft from the great ship's engine room blowers that lifted her momentarily, just long enough to half-arrest the trainer's shallow death dive.

The aircraft rolled back and beyond the horizontal and then for the first time in half-a-dozen terrifying seconds which had seemed to stretch for infinity, Alex had the trainer back under control.

He risked a look forward.

His passenger was still in her seat in the front cockpit.

Jesus and Mary, I do not want to do that again!

Only then did he start to ask: what just happened?

He eased back the stick to gain a little altitude; when in doubt H-E-I-G-H-T always spells S-A-F-E-T-Y!

Where was all the smoke coming from?

Heck, it was as hazy as Hades on a bad day...

Two holes the size of his fist suddenly opened up on his bottom right wing.

'What the..."

He recognised bullet holes when he saw them!

Who the fuck was shooting at him!

He pushed the throttle hard forward, climbing, climbing and then he looked back, at first over his shoulder but when he did not believe the evidence of his eyes he rolled the trainer into a long turn so that he could have a proper look at the surreal scene of utter mayhem in the Upper Bay.

Chapter 25

HMS Cassandra, Upper Bay, New York

"Might I suggest you step below, Your Majesty?" The destroyer's captain suggested respectfully as the ship's bell - piped at ear-splitting decibel levels over the ship's speakers – sent men sprinting for their battle stations and the barrels of the forward main battery guns began to seek prey.

King George had had binoculars glued to his eyes for the last thirty seconds as he tried to make out what was going on around the Lions of the 5th Battle Squadron.

"The Flagship is broadcasting in the plain, sir!" A yeoman called urgently.

"Put it on the bridge circuit!"

"Princess Royal and Queen Elizabeth are under attack by motor launches and aircraft. Cassandra is to run for the Lower Bay at best speed and shelter with the Formidables!"

The King was having none of that nonsense.

"Inform C-in-C 5th Battle Squadron that the King of England runs from no man!" He declaimed irritably. This said he reconsidered, looking to his wife. "Eleanor, my love, perhaps you might step below until this unpleasantness is resolved."

"I will do no such thing, Bertie!"

Everybody on the bridge was donning heavy bullet proof jackets – the naval version was a part life jacket, part anti-flash version of the army and police 'combat garment' – and the royal couple realised that they and Henrietta De L'Isle were expected to do likewise if they were to remain in situ.

"Oh really!" The King complained.

"I'm not wearing one of those things unless you do, Bertie!" His wife decided.

Henrietta positively sagged beneath the weight of her jacket.

Eleanor was escorted to the captain's chair where she gratefully took the twenty-four pounds of extra weight off her feet.

The King allowed men to check his 'suit of armour' was correctly clamped about his torso while tin hats were presented to his wife and the Governor's youngest daughter.

While all this was going on Cassandra had slowed to a crawl and a dozen lookouts and officers had been attempting to fathom what was actually going on a mile or so to the north.

The destroyer's captain reported to his sovereign.

"Sir Thomas has said that I am to obey your orders, sir," he said. "His words were: 'He's the bloody King and he outranks me'," he went on. "Sir," he finished with a wan smile.

The King waved at the smoke-filled Upper Bay.

"Take us up there and tell Guns to blow anything that blinks at us to pieces!"

"Aye, aye, sir!" In a moment HMS Cassandra was surging forward like a greyhound out of the traps.

In the distance HMS Princess Royal was on fire.

Momentarily, it seemed to those on Cassandra's bridge that the third ship in line, the Queen Elizabeth's after fifteen-inch guns had fired a salvo but then, when their brains had had time to process the evidence of their eyes they realised that what they had seen was an aircraft crashing into the battleship's aftermost turret.

There was a huge splash of fire.

An aircraft, a Bristol VI with a silvery fuselage raced past the now charging destroyer heading, obviously for the stern of the Tiger, the fourth ship in the battle line.

The Gunnery Officer's voice boomed over the bridge speakers.

"ALL GUNS THAT BEAR TO ENGAGE FAST MOVING TARGET BEARING GREEN ZERO-THREE-ZERO!

WEAPONS FREE IN LOCAL CONTROL! REPEAT WEAPONS FREE IN LOCAL CONTROL!"

The destroyer reverberated with the recoil of her two aft 4.7-inch guns, shortly followed by the chain-saw rattling of her quick-firing quadruple 0.8-inch cannons.

The 4.7-inch rounds went over the approaching speed boat. It was already too close for the main battery barrels to depress sufficiently to engage it.

The boat was bright red, nearly crimson and approaching at breakneck speed. Every detail of the onrushing craft was suddenly clearly visible despite the fog of war now hanging over the water like a rapidly spreading evil miasma. It was as if the speedboat was cleaving aside the haze. As cannon shells tore into the water and ricocheted haphazardly yachts and launches were heading every which way desperately trying to escape...whatever was happening.

The quadruple 0.8 cannons, each barrel shooting at a rate of over two-hundred and fifty rounds a minute – ripped up the sea ahead of the blood-red wraith screaming, almost skimming across the waves impossibly fast – until the stream of cannon shells intersected with the frail craft and it disintegrated in a thousand disarticulated, spinning, splashing fragments.

Up ahead the Bristol VI heading doggedly for the Tiger was smoking heavily, clearly on the verge of falling out of the sky. No gun on the Cassandra dared to fire for fear of raking the decks of the battleship.

The King gripped the bridge rail in nameless, impotent rage as the aircraft, trailing a plume of burning gasoline across the smoke fouled air fell onto the quarterdeck of the leviathan and disintegrating, tumbled fierily until it met the immovable armoured obstacle of the battleship's 'Y' 15-inch turret.

And exploded.

Chapter 26

HMS Lion, Upper Bay, New York

By the time the big ships had brought all their light weaponry – essentially, their 1.7 and 0.8-inch twin and quadruple anti-aircraft mounts – into play the sky had cleared of aircraft and every small boat in the bay was running for cover.

Rear Admiral Sir Thomas Packenham drew breath knowing that right now he needed to be the calmest man in New England. His flagship was the only one of the four Lions to have escaped unscathed; and although reports were streaming in from Princess Royal, Queen Elizabeth, Tiger and the cruisers Ajax and Naiad, still guarding Lion's flanks, none of his big ships had suffered critical damage.

Right at the beginning of the attack – which thus far had lasted some twelve minutes, starting to peter out after about eight – a big speedboat had smashed into Princess Royal's starboard side abreast her bridge. An unknown number of men who had been manning the rail had perished and many must have been injured as the lightweight speedster had disintegrated against the 13-inch cemented armour plating protecting that part of the hull above and below the waterline.

More serious had been the aircraft which had smashed into the rear of the Princess Royal's bridge and started a fire which had destroyed a pair of 1.7-inch cannon mounts, wiping out their crews and igniting adjacent ready-use ammunition lockers.

Astern of Princess Royal the Queen Elizabeth had been rammed by two speed boats, and by an aircraft which had crashed between the barbettes of the aft 'X' and 'Y' main battery turrets. This latter strike had barely scratched the fourteen-inch thick armour protecting the turrets but a large explosive charge in the bow of one of the boats had opened a ten feet wide hole in the less heavily armoured stern plating and about six hundred tons of water had flooded into two compartments initially causing a list to port of slightly less than one degree.

Tiger had sustained a single aircraft strike which had scorched her quarterdeck and damaged the range-finder of her 'Y' 15-inch turret.

Ships specifically designed to withstand hits by two-ton 15-inch shells plunging onto, into and around them at supersonic speeds, and one-thousand-pound armour-piercing bombs dropped from aircraft flying at five thousand feet, had not been meaningfully inconvenienced by motor boats displacing at most a few tons 'bumping' into their mightily robust and armour-encased sides like explosive dodgem cars, or small, fragile aircraft crumpling up on their decks. Notwithstanding the fact that most of the aircraft involved seemed to have been virtual flying petrol cans – which was a nasty twist - apart from Princess Royal's problem with ready-use ammunition catching fire, all the resultant fires had swiftly burned out, or been expeditiously extinguished by damage control teams.

Had the Lions not been 'dressing the side' with hundreds of men on parade on deck at the outset of the attack casualties would have been minimal.

"Cassandra is hailing us, sir!"

The fleet destroyer had raced into the midst of the action, now with her screws churning astern she slewed to a near halt between the Naiad and the Lion, the signal lamp on her port bridge wing flashing furiously.

In the near distance 0.8 and 1.7-inch ammunition lit off like fireworks and smoke billowed downwind to the south east from the superstructure of the Princess Royal.

Tom Packenham did not wait for a yeoman to call out Cassandra's signal.

He chuckled to himself.

"WELL DONE EVERYBODY STOP THERE WILL BE HELL TO PAY WHEN WE FIND OUT WHO IS BEHIND IT STOP QUEEN AND I STILL IN ONE PIECE STOP I WILL REMAIN ON CASSANDRA UNTIL SITUATION CLEAR STOP GEORGE V MESSAGE ENDS"

The Squadron Commander was about to swap jocular small talk with the Lion's captain when both men heard HMS Ajax's quadruple 1.7-inch mounts angrily clatter back into life.

That was when they heard the sound of the two aircraft approaching.

Chapter 27

Upper Bay, New York

Alex Fielding had flown over Bedford Island and on into New Jersey and circled south over Elizabethtown at about three thousand feet. He would have searched for somewhere to land but after what he had just witnessed in the bay an unfamiliar aircraft was liable to be shot at. Fortunately, he had plenty of fuel left in the tank so he could afford to stooge around and wait for things to settle down.

All the other times he had been in the air in the middle of a battle he had had the comfort of knowing he had a couple of machine guns mounted either on his kite's nose or top wing; so, in the last few minutes he had felt positively naked.

He had no real sense of time passing; he was too busy scanning the skies around him and trying to piece together the insanity of the last few minutes.

That Bristol VI which hit the last battleship in line had looked an awful lot like one of the ones Magnus McIntyre and Paul Hopkins had been flying. And by the size of the fireball it must have been carrying spare cans of 87-octane or some kind of explosive charge onboard when it hit...

Oh shit!

That would explain why those comedians had taken such long take-off runs...

This just got worse!

Guess who signed their temporary Long Island Flying Certificates?

No, no, no he was letting his imagination get the better of his brain.

Every amateur flier in New England was snapping up Bristol Vs and VIs for a song as the CAF re-quipped with modern types; hardly any of the idiots who bought those kites knew how to fly the things. The lunatics crashing their rides into those ships did not even need to know how to land the damned things!

Although, the question of exactly what sort of a man would deliberately crash his kite, let alone deliberately crash it onto the deck of a battleship defied all reason.

You would have to be insane?

Wouldn't you?

The big ships were alone in the Bay; all the small craft had scuttled for cover with their crews waving anything they could find that was remotely white as they got out of the firing line. From the amount of debris and fuel oil fouling the Upper Bay a lot of innocent people must have been caught in the cross fire. He noticed for the first time that the third battleship in the line had started leaking a new, thin slick of black bunker oil into the dirty grey waters downstream towards Hell's Gate.

A pillar of black, grey-streaked smoke was billowing from the second battleship in line from somewhere amidships. The pall of smoke was drifting east across Red Hook. Periodically there were flashes, pinpricks of light through the increasing murk of the fog of war. That would be ammunition exploding, small stuff, nothing that was going to sink a ship like that.

Alex was about to point his aircraft south over Staten Island and begin a long, circular return to Jamaica Bay when he saw the other aircraft.

A Bristol VI.

Well, he did not so much see it as collide with it!

It almost flew straight into him!

He threw the stick to the right and for a moment looked the man at the controls of the other machine in the eye.

Rufus McIntyre...

Chapter 28

Brooklyn Heights, Long Island

Colonel Matthew Harrison had had his driver take him up to a vantage point on Brooklyn Heights to join the crowds gawking at the big ships anchored in the main channel less than a couple of miles away. Even at that distance the four Lions looked damned big, utterly indestructible, the very foundations of the Empire.

The Governor of the Commonwealth of New England was going to give him a hard time about John Watson. It was not going to be enough to rely on the line that he was shot resisting arrest, those nincompoops had filled him so full of lead, front and back, that he was going to have to throw them all to the wolves.

Heck, that was the sort of thing criminals did to each other, not honest to God patriotic CSS Agents!

What was it they said about no plan surviving contact with the enemy?

Inevitably, when you designed an operation with as many moving parts as *Empire Day* it was to be expected that not everything would work out the way it was supposed to and that somewhere along the line somebody was going to have to be thrown under the train.

Nonetheless, he was still a little disappointed that Sarah had not been able to tie down the Sons of Liberty angle; even though that had always been a speculative exercise, just another level of insurance in case something went badly wrong elsewhere. A lot of people were going to want somebody to take the rap – and probably swing from a gibbet – in the coming months and it was going to be as hard as Hell to pin it on the real bad guys.

The real bad guys!

What was going on out there in the Upper Bay was *effect*

not *cause*. The men in those speedboats and aircraft crashing into the symbols of Imperial dominion honestly believed that they were martyrs doing God's sacred work.

Were they the bad guys?

What about the men whose negligence and complacency had brought the First Thirteen to their knees?

In any event, most of the men the papers and those smart-arsed college boys on TV would call the evildoers would soon be – if they were not already – dead out there in the fires and smoke blanketing much of the Upper Bay. They had fulfilled their role in the tragedy of the age; now it was for others to pick up the flag.

It was frustrating being able to see so little. The folks up on the top, road deck, of the Brooklyn-Manhattan bridge would have had the best view looking down to the south from two hundred feet above the East River. The head of the CSS had contemplated joining them up there, decided against it. He instinctively mistrusted hubris even when a plan had come together so perfectly.

Perfection, of course, was a relative thing.

He would have a better feel for the post-outrage situation when he learned who had lived and who had died. In the confusion fall guys as well as actors would have died or been taken prisoner and as with any conspiracy the key thing was for everybody to get their story straight at the outset.

That, and to make damned sure one had a cast of scapegoats and hapless victims who just happened to be in the wrong place at the wrong time. Harrison hated loose ends; like for example, where in the name of Hades was the youngest Fielding boy? He had been promised he would be in the air over the bay today but the latest he had heard was that the kid had gone off up country with his little squaw!

That just was not natural!

There were good reasons why that sort of thing was illegal in the northern colonies!

It was bad enough the whole population along the South West border gradually turning a dusky shade of white. In a way that was understandable; the Border War had turned that whole region into a racial melting pot but nobody gave a damn about that because West Texas, the disputed Coahuila, Nuevo Mexico and Alta California borderlands were so far from anywhere remotely civilised that decent folk back in the First Thirteen colonies were not about to get offended. Up here in the North East people had standards. People had a right to expect dedicated public servants like him to defend their God-given beliefs and prerogatives, and when necessary to try his Christian conscience to its limit to ensure that God's work continued to be done in the Commonwealth of New England. The rest of the Empire could go to Hell in a handcart if it wanted to depart from the path of the Lord; here in the heartland of the First Thirteen there would be no compromise, no surrender to the godless, libertarian excesses so common elsewhere in what ought to be for all time the White Empire.

Nonetheless, it saddened him that so many undoubtedly good, innocent people had suffered on this auspicious bicentenary of that original act of shameless, unmitigated treachery in Philadelphia in 1776.

His country had needed to be shocked out of its complacency before it sleep-walked too far down the road to perdition. And, if in the process he had evened up a few old scores well, that was just the way things were.

If the English had taught the peoples of the Empire anything it was that the victors always got to write the first draft of history.

The people around Harrison had fallen silent.

Now they began to stir anew.

The crackle of heavy automatic gunfire rumbled anew across the Upper Bay.

Chapter 29

East Islip, Suffolk County, Long Island

To be frank I had no idea what I was actually watching until I saw the cameras zeroing in on HMS Princess Royal to catch the moment when one of her ready use ammunition lockers blew up and Sarah finally turned up the sound.

"This is going on right now," she informed me just when I thought nothing could possibly ever surprise me ever again.

I am not sure what she expected me to say; not unnaturally I was speechless. I had been frog-marched down a corridor and up a flight of stairs by two brawny military types – although they were not actually in uniform, they just had that look about them – whose general demeanour was that of men who would much rather be beating me to a pulp than hanging onto my arms to stop me falling over.

The TV had already been on in the lounge – it had a settee, a couple of comfortable chairs, a low table for tea things, so I reckoned it was a lounge no matter that it was in a CSS interrogation centre – and I had been bundled into one of the chairs. I stared, mostly in horror at what I was watching.

"This started happening a few minutes ago," Sarah added with a nasty 'I told you so' inflexion. "But you already know that!"

There was a clock on the wall.

It indicated that it was 11:13, presumably in the morning.

"What do you mean? I know about precisely nothing to do with that!"

I gesticulated angrily at the screen.

By then I would have been hard-pressed to confidently

say what day it actually was...

I was a little disappointed that the CSS did not have a colour television; sure, they were very expensive but the CSS was always the last colonial department to feel the pinch when it came to saving the pennies.

The picture was a little grainy and juddered periodically as if the cameraman was as shaken as everybody else watching the transmission. Suddenly, pictures from a new angle were on screen. The lens swung about the sky, steadied and zoomed in on two aircraft, still distant but in a shallow dive. This camera was not on a small launch bobbing around in the Bay but on the rock-steady deck of a big warship.

"I don't think any of the Lion's guns will bear on these two!" This from a breathless commentator more used to covering football or rugby matches. *"No, no... That's the flagship's forward 1.7-inch guns starting up..."*

At that moment the man's voice was entirely drowned out by the air-ripping hammering of a nearby quadruple anti-aircraft mount. The cameraman must have jumped out of his skin because the lens was suddenly jerked to the right looking down the port superstructure of one of the Navy's heavy cruisers.

Cordite smoke drifted, briefly obscuring the view and when it cleared the cacophony was crackling, overwhelming the TV microphones as spent cartridge cases spewed onto the nearby deck.

The camera swung away again.

The commentator was shouting; his voice hoarse and breaking with his impossible excitement, and presumably, no little fear.

"There they are! There they are! My God, they almost collided! Goodness knows how they haven't been shot down yet..."

Even from the shaky TV pictures on the twenty-four-inch

screen in the CSS lounge I could see that the Lion and by now several other ships were filling the air *ahead* of the two old-fashioned, relatively slow biplanes with hot metal and exploding shells but that hardly any of the growing volume of fire was actually passing anywhere near them.

"THEY ALMOST COLLIDED AGAIN!"

I blinked, unable to make sense of it.

Any of it.

The leading aircraft – it looked like a Bristol VI, one of the sportster versions that was so popular ten years ago when air racing first became so fashionable – ought to have been showing its companion a clean pair of heels.

The second plane, a much older Bristol V, doped canvas all over without the VI's partially stressed-aluminium fuselage streamlining had swooped so close that the leading aircraft had had to veer away to the left.

Now the two aircraft were coming together again.

"It is almost as if the second plane is trying to knock the leading one out of the sky!"

Sarah stepped in front of the screen and instinctively I shifted in my chair to look around her.

"I hope you're pleased with yourself, Isaac?"

Although my captors had given me water I had not eaten since I could not remember when, I was light-headed from hunger, and more than somewhat knocked about and bruised.

I was NOT particularly pleased about anything at that moment!

I lost my temper.

"What the fuck are you talking about?" I inquired, more testily than I meant.

Sarah gestured at the mostly concealed screen.

"All this!" She hissed venomously. "This is all your work. Your work and the work of the Sons of Liberty!"

I would have snapped back something witty, pithy in fact

had I not been so stunned. Stunned very much, in fact, in the manner I might have been had I just been brained with a cricket bat.

Consequently, I did not begin to start fully processing what my – clearly ex-common law wife – had accused me of until I was being bundled, al la sack of potatoes into my cell with the metallic clunking of the door being slammed shut behind me ringing in my ears.

I hardly had the energy or the will to get off my knees. It seemed simpler to roll over on my back and to stare up at the ceiling so that was what I did.

Despite the mountain of evidence to the contrary I think I had still believed, right up until then, that I would be able to talk my way out of this. I always had before; but now I was reluctantly coming to the ineluctable conclusion that this was one of those scrapes where being the smartest guy in the room was not going to cut it.

This was different.

This time that bastard Matthew Harrison had got all the angles covered!

Chapter 30

Upper Bay, New York

Leonora Coolidge had never, ever been so exhilarated. Utterly terrified also but as she clung to the leather rim of the forward cockpit of the old Bristol V as it swooped and juddered, threatening to shake itself to pieces towards the wall of exploding shells and the impenetrable wall of tracers, it was as if she was outside of her body looking down on the unfolding drama.

When her pilot had swung the aircraft back towards the ships in the Upper Bay she had, for a fraction of a second wondered if she had hitched a ride with a member of the gang of lunatics who had already crashed several machines into one or other of the battleships far below; but then she had realised her mistake.

Her pilot might be a madman but he was not one of the bad guys. First, he had attempted to fly alongside the other aircraft, one of the shiny, more modern models of the string-bag in which she was riding, and insanely, he had attempted to flip it over using his left-hand top wing-tip. Secondly, when that failed he had veered straight towards the other aircraft and come within a whisker of sawing off his tail with his propeller.

As if that was not surreal what was going on now was too incredible for belief!

The man in the Bristol VI doggedly heading for the northernmost battleship in the Upper Bay was periodically looking over his shoulder and firing a pistol at them!

Should I duck?

No, I might miss something!

It was probably the benefit of the two Martinis she had downed before she set off for Jamaica Field that morning but bizarrely, the faster this crazy roller coaster went the less she got distracted by minor considerations such as: am I about to die?

She had never been so alive, her senses were so electrically, ecstatically heightened that she was aware of *everything* going on around her in pinpoint detail.

The aircraft juddered to the right, recovered.

Leonora craned her neck to look around.

The pilot had blood on his face and grim determination in his eyes as if he was looking through her.

When next she focused on the other aircraft it was almost close enough to touch.

They were going to ram it!

In a second it would all be over.

Should I shut my eyes?

No, it will hurt as much either way!

The Bristol V wobbled and bucked in the slipstream of the leading aircraft and suddenly Leonora was looking beyond it; she gasped when she saw how close they were to the leading battleship.

It seemed so huge it filled the world...

Momentarily, the vortex of bursting shells and criss-crossing machine-gun fire which had stubbornly remained fifty or a hundred yards ahead of the two planes rushed towards and enveloped them both.

For a split second both aircraft were within the firestorm.

Leonora felt the Bristol V staggering, lurching sidelong, bouncing with impossible violence. She heard metal and wooden spars splintering. The machine lurched sidelong and then she was in clear air.

The aircraft's motor spat gouts of smoke from its exhausts and seized and the sea rushed up towards her impossibly fast

Chapter 31

HMS Lion, Upper Bay, New York

Rear Admiral Sir Thomas Packenham watched the approaching aircraft with cool professional detachment. Every forward facing anti-aircraft gun was shooting at the two fragile Bristol scouts, and to the left and the right both the Ajax and the Naiad were filling the sky with metal, too. And yet the two old machines still came on, wobbling through the turbulence of the exploding ordnance seemingly invulnerable.

"Our bloody guns are shooting short!" He complained.

The problem would lie with the variables programmed into his ships' gun control tables. Neither of the oncoming aircraft could achieve anywhere near the default one hundred and fifty mile an hour minimum speed set up on the high angle air defence directors. None of these blighters would have laid a finger on his ships if somebody had had the wit to alter the parameters. It was too late now; thank God these string bags were so flimsy they crumpled up the moment they hit one of his leviathans.

Problematically, there was going to be the mother and father of all inquests – or rather, inquisitions – when this was over. Thus far three of the Royal Navy's most modern battleships had been damaged, granted not seriously, by a bunch of maniacs in speed boats and fifteen to twenty-year old obsolete biplanes and the one thing the Admiralty never, ever tolerated was being made to look stupid.

Dammit, what would have happened if the King or the Queen had been injured? The Commander of the 5th Battle Squadron shook his head, wincing at the very thought. Literally, he would have fallen on his sword. Or, more likely borrowed somebody's service pistol rather than attempted that barbaric Japanese Seppuku, hari-kari ritual, he was

British after all.

As it was his fate was probably going to be significantly messier.

The King would do his best to lessen the blow but he knew his old friend too well to know that he would not overtly intervene in the Court of Inquiry which would inevitably recommend that he, the Squadron Commander, the man in charge of this fiasco, be court-martialled.

As Tom Packenham gazed around the Upper Bay and the sporadic detonations of more of the Princess Royal's ready use anti-aircraft shells crackled across the smoky waters he wondered if the word 'fiasco' even began to do justice to the humiliation and the outrage that today's events would invoke across the whole Empire.

"We've got one of them!" Somebody nearby on the open flying bridge atop Lion's armoured bridge cried more in relief than triumph.

Packenham saw one aircraft slewing to port with what looked like pieces of wing and fuselage falling off it trailing grey smoke shot through with streaks of crimson fire gliding towards the stone-coloured waters of the Bay.

The other aircraft was on fire.

It was heading straight at him.

Men around him began to scurry for cover as the Bristol VI wobbled over the Lion's bow. The big quadruple 1.7-inch automatic cannons no longer bore on the aircraft but heavy machine guns and rifles, in the hands of Royal Marines still resplendent in their ceremonial redcoats dressing the rails and standing on the two forward 15-inch main battery turrets, were knocking lumps out of the scout, which it seemed must disintegrate at any moment.

But Tom Packenham knew that was not going to happen.

He stood rigidly to attention.

The last thing he saw in this life was the blur of the spinning propeller a microsecond before it, the wreck of the

Bristol VI, thirty gallons of 87-octane gasoline and the one hundred and sixty-seven pounds of dynamite inside the bullet-riddled fuselage of the biplane crashed into and detonated squarely against the binnacle platform in the middle of the flying bridge.

Chapter 32

Mohawk Valley, New York

The small group paddled two miles up-river, keeping out of the main stream, hugging the banks where the slow-moving water eddied and swirled before hauling the boats onto land and loading them onto the ancient flatbed, much-modified rusting Leyland lorry Tsiokwaris had used to transport first Kate, and then himself and his nephews to this southerly part of the tribal grounds in the previous days. Abe and Kate squeezed into the cab with the old man, the teenage boys rode with the canoes as the charabanc wheezed and coughed down over-grown and unmaintained roads through the narrow breaks in the wilderness that barely qualified as tracks.

The Albany to Buffalo trunk road, likewise the railway still ran through Mohawk land north of the river but all the latter's branch lines had been abandoned, like the tarmac roads which used to quarter the forests a quarter of a century ago and were slowly being reclaimed by nature.

Here and there the Leyland bumped and jolted past derelict farmsteads; the cabins that hunters and fishermen from the towns and cities once used to frequent in summer had mostly been vandalised, their roofs pulled down or simply torched by their owners when the colony's bailiffs came calling. That had been one of the many unforeseen consequences of the rigid application – county by county – of the *Getrennte Entwicklung* policies of the forties and fifties. A lot of colonists, including most of the small farmers had tried to hang on as long as possible and even as recently as ten or fifteen years ago illegal hunting and trapping had been a big problem in these lands. Nothing happened all at once, and the ideologues of separate development had remorselessly tightened the law until the penalties for breaking its legal straightjacket were as severe, possibly more so, for white colonists than for the 'natives'. So, these days nobody maintained the roads and land cleared for arable rotation had gone back to nature as the forest began swallow up the fields.

The Mohawks had no need for great ribbons of concrete across their lands, the great river was their highway, its creeks and tributaries their by-roads and border markers. Motor vehicles were increasingly rare deep in the forests; whatever was needed for the common good, food staples, medicines and fuel for generators, spare parts for the old machines in the handful of factories still operating in the hinterland all came up, or down the seasonally moody waterway in its heart. That the river froze over in winter, was unnavigable in the spring until the ice had melted, flooded and was effectively closed to traffic for half the year was of no matter; the People of the Flint understood as much and lived their lives accordingly, in tune with the whims and the boons of the seasons.

Understandably, more than one kind of exile or fugitive sought sanctuary in Iroquois country and Tsiokwaris's people did not extend the hand of friendship to every manner of interloper. That could be cruel for although this land could seem like a new Eden this was a harsh country for the unwary, the city-born and bred for whom 'living off the forest' was as unrealistic as it was foolhardy.

It was mid-day by the time the Leyland ground to a halt in the foothills of the Adirondack Mountains on the northern slopes of the Mohawk Valley overlooking what had once been the village of St Johnsville. Like so many communities in the valley it had briefly boomed when the order had come from Government House in Philadelphia to drive a ship canal from Lake Erie down the valley – which bisected the Catskill Mountains to the south and the Adirondacks to the north – all the way to the Hudson River. But when the money ran out in the 1860s the half-finished 'great trench' was forgotten and with it, a dozen places like St Johnsville.

Several long log dwellings were arranged randomly in the trees on the high side of a babbling brook whose course down to the valley was interrupted by the derelict mill ponds of the district's first European settlers. Now the creeks fell down the hillsides in a series of small artificial waterfalls from one crumbling dyke to another, and here and there fallen trees had formed additional temporary low weirs.

The Iroquois had robbed out the stones of the settler cottages and mill-houses for the foundations for their cabins and to make permanent paths through the trees and across the boggy down slopes adjacent to the creek.

The settlers had cleared the land either side of the waterway; now the forest was growing back, reclaiming its banks and the log long houses almost seemed like a part of the land.

This place would be almost invisible from the air...

Abe found himself being introduced to a dozen aunts, uncles, nieces, nephews and cousins most of whom he had never met. He caught a few words in Kanien'kehaka, smiled and nodded his head acknowledging each new smiling face.

Hopefully, his ear would quickly attune to voices and inflexions other than Kate's, allowing him to begin to understand what was being said to him.

His wife had warned him that few of her people 'in the forest' understood or spoke English and that few of her tribe had ever troubled to learn to read or write. In her own land Tsiokwaris was viewed as something of an eccentric – still very respected – elder for still insisting that every member of his immediate family was literate in the White Man's tongue.

Getrennte Entwicklung was a thing that cut both ways.

For many in the Iroquois Nation it was a blessing to be cut off from the infernal noise and confusion of the colonial world; to be saved from the bizarre religious conventions of the cities and to be able to live again as their ancestors had lived.

Presently, Kate drew Abe aside.

They sat on a rock staring into the waters of the creek tumbling gently down to the valley.

"What are you thinking?" Kate asked.

"I thought I'd be more afraid," Abe replied.

"Me too," she confessed.

ACT III – THE DAY AFTER

Monday 5th July 1976

Chapter 33

HMS Lion, Upper Bay, New York

The King was in a grim frame of mind. He and his wife had visited the battleship's sick bay that morning before returning to what had been Rear Admiral Sir Thomas Packenham's day cabin to chair the meeting which would determine whether or not the New England leg of the forthcoming Royal Tour went ahead.

However, first he had received the casualty and damage reports from Rear Admiral Christopher Trowbridge, the Commander of the First Cruiser Squadron.

Trowbridge was a direct descendant of one of Nelson's band of brothers, a tall, hawk-browed man nearing retirement under whom the King had once served as a junior gunnery officer back in the late 1940s.

"Queen Elizabeth will need to proceed to Norfolk to dry dock for repairs, sir. At a pinch she could steam at twenty-four or five knots and hold her station in the battle line. Princess Royal's upper deck is a bit of a mess but again, a week or two in dockyard hands will see her as good as new. Tiger's damage is superficial, a few scorched deck planks. Repairs on 'Y' turret's range-finders will be completed within forty-eight hours." Trowbridge paused, sucked his teeth.

"Lion is fully operational. Negligible structural damage was caused to her bridge superstructure by the crash of that small aeroplane yesterday. The ship's company expects to have cleared all debris and recovered the bodies of the dead this day. Repairs will be completed in the next twenty-four hours."

Of the four Lions, only the Tiger had suffered no casualties.

Princess Royal reported seventeen dead, two missing and thirty-nine injured. Queen Mary had twenty-eight dead and four men missing, and another fifty-one injured. Lion had sustained fifteen dead and eleven seriously injured.

"We now believe that at least six aircraft and as many fast motor launches or speedboats attempted to crash into one or other of the Lions," Trowbridge continued grimly. Of these; four aircraft and four boats succeeded in their suicide missions. The survivors of the second aircraft which attacked the Lion are presently being held under guard in the sick bay. There were no other survivors from these attacks."

Queen Eleanor coughed genteelly.

At the beginning of his reign her husband's predilection for inviting her to sit in on his tête-à-têtes with his closest advisors and courtiers had put a lot of noses out of joint. Nowadays, her presence rarely raised an eyebrow. In fact, it often calmed otherwise heated situations and made it easier for everybody to remember their manners and to keep their passions in hand.

"What of casualties among the civilian fleet, Admiral Trowbridge?" She inquired quietly. "All those poor people who found themselves caught, through no fault of their own, in the cross fire?"

"We believe that as many as a dozen craft may have been hit and some twenty persons may have died or gone into the water or been injured. Our rescue boats recovered some two dozen persons from the water yesterday, all bar one of whom was alive at that point, Ma'am."

The King looked to the stocky, moustachioed brooding presence of the Head of the Colonial Security Service, Colonel Matthew Harrison. The man's Lincoln Green uniform sat uneasily on his large frame.

"I believe that the man you suspect to have been behind that dreadful business at Wallabout Bay on Saturday was shot and killed in the process of being apprehended by your people?"

Harrison shifted uncomfortably in his chair.

"Yes, Your Majesty..."

"Damned unfortunate!"

"Yes..."

"But you have others implicated in recent events in custody, I gather?"

"Yes, Your Majesty." Harrison swallowed hard. He glanced to the impassive figure of the Governor of the Commonwealth of New England, Viscount De L'Isle, who was sitting next to him before continuing: "We've been attempting to infiltrate and to keep under close observation a subversive, terroristic organisation called the Sons of Liberty for some time, Your Majesty. Legally, you appreciate, our powers of arrest and our ability to maintain close surveillance of suspect individuals is limited..."

The King scowled impatiently.

"Yes, well whatever the provocation the Empire won't have any truck with police state methods!"

"No, of course not..."

The King realised he was allowing his outrage to colour his judgements. It did not help that within the last hour he had had to peremptorily reject both his Prime Minister's and the First Lord of the Admiralty's offers to resign their posts. At a time like this the ship needed all hands manning the pumps!

"I apologise, Colonel Harrison," the King grunted. "Please, you were saying..."

"We attempted to round up the leading members of the Sons of Liberty ahead of the Empire Day celebrations," Harrison went on. "We have for some time suspected that the guiding hand behind the organisation is a certain Isaac Putnam Fielding, who operates under the cover of being a somewhat dissolute Professor of History at Long Island College. The man who was rescued from the aircraft that crashed into the sea after attempting and failing to attack the Lion is his eldest son, Alexander. We have yet to establish the precise role of his accomplice, a Leonora Coolidge..."

"They are the pair under guard in the sick bay presumably?"

Harrison belatedly recollected that the Governor had told him: 'First you will address the King as *Your Majesty*, and thereafter, simply as *Sir.*'

"Yes, sir."

"You say you have this Isaac Fielding fellow in custody?"

"Yes, sir. The man who was killed resisting arrest on Friday night was his son-in-law. We have not yet established the involvement or culpability of his wife, Fielding's daughter Victoria who is seriously ill at Queen Mary's Hospital in Brooklyn. Overnight we arrested Fielding's second son, William, who works at the Gowanus Cove workshops of the Long Island Speedboat Company. We have also put out a Colony-wide warrant for the arrest of Fielding's youngest son, Abraham. Like his brother Alexander, Abraham Fielding was a pilot so it is not beyond the bounds of possibility that he was piloting one of the planes which crashed into the battleships."

Eleanor was horrified.

"A whole family of terrorists? What would make them all do such a terrible thing?"

"We believe that Isaac Fielding, who many years ago was the author of a seditious tract called," Matthew Harrison grimaced apologetically, as did Viscount De L'Isle, "*Two Hundred Lost Years: What the World might have looked like if George Washington had ducked at the right time...*"

The Governor of New England stirred.

"I gather that attempts were made to prosecute various persons associated with the book but thirty or more years ago the best advice available to my esteemed predecessor was that quote: 'freedom of speech means exactly that'. Moreover, at the time according to the papers I have seen, this man Fielding was viewed as a harmless, frankly whimsical pacifistic crank."

Having made this observation De L'Isle nodded for the security chief to carry on.

Harrison collected his wits.

"As unlikely as it seems we believe that over the years Fielding indoctrinated and radicalised his children, poisoning their young minds against the Crown. Latterly, there is evidence that in league with a Puritan faction called the Brethren of the Mayflower Fielding abandoned non-violence in favour of well," he shrugged, "the madness we witnessed yesterday."

The King absorbed this.

"Thank you, Colonel Harrison. On your return ashore please convey my personal thanks and appreciation to your people for the courageous, and I know, sometimes onerous work they do in the service of the Commonwealth of New England."

Harrison bowed his head.

"Thank you, sir."

"Now," the monarch went on. "We must turn to the question of what to do next. The 'security response' to the events of the last hours will be a matter to be determined by My Government and its agent in New England, Viscount De

L'Isle."

The King had learned very quickly that there was no minute or hour of any day when he was not His Majesty George the Fifth, by the Grace of God of the United Kingdom of Great Britain and Northern Ireland and of His Other Realms and Territories King, Head of the Commonwealth, Defender of the Faith.

However, it was also true to say that there were often times when his people required him to be more *George V, Dei Gratia Britanniarum Regnorumque Suorum Ceterorum Rex, Consortionis Populorum Princeps, Fidei Defensor* than ever!

This was one such moment.

"The Queen and I have discussed the subject of our forthcoming progress through New England and determined that it will proceed as planned."

He reached out and took his wife's hand.

"Just so there is no debate about this," the King added bluntly, "this is *our* irrevocable decision. This is *my* last word on the subject."

Chapter 34

Mohawk Valley, New York

Abe had not realised how much he was going to enjoy sleeping with – actually, just sleeping with – Kate. They had never really done much of that in the past other than occasional post-coital pauses for breath. This morning had been the third dawn in a row he had awakened with his wife in his arms and...*it was so damned nice.*

To tell the truth he was still in a little bit of a daze; a lot of stuff had not sunken in yet. He and Kate had been married within the Mohawk Nation three years ago but that had simply been promises in Kanien'kehá:ka that Abe had barely understood at the time; words exchanged among his second family in a small gathering of elders and Kate's female relations. Her mother had died when she was young so her aunts had always been her 'mothers'; and Tsiokwaris had married or lived as man and wife with the senior aunt Skawennahawi – which translated roughly as 'she who carries the message' – an arrangement which Abe had never really got his head around but that did not matter, it had worked well for Kate and that was the important thing.

In any event 'the aunts' had organised a proper tribal wedding shindig and people had begun to fill the settlement that morning as the preparations went ahead.

Last night he and Kate had gone up the valley side, found a mossy spot and laid down to stare up at the slow-moving theatre of the starry night. Out here so far from the urban sprawl of Albany, the nearest big city, the air was crystal clear and the great sweep of the Milky Way fell across the heavens like a broad band of distant diamonds.

This morning there were several aircraft flying up and down the Mohawk River, one flew directly over the settlement and headed north.

Kate nudged him gently in the ribs.

The 'celebrations' were about to commence.

No time had been set; the party would simply begin when a consensus was reached among the 'aunts' that the moment was propitious.

"Those are military planes," Abe murmured. He was standing just inside the tree line looking down into the valley trying to quell the uneasiness in his soul. Most of the aerial activity seemed to be some miles south, down river. If Kate and he had still been on Leppe Island those machines would be buzzing over their heads all the time!

"I thought today was supposed to be a white man's holiday?" His wife teased him, on the verge of giggling. Kate had been giggling a lot since they had arrived. She never made any attempt to hide it when she was happy.

True, today was the Empire Day Holiday; the whole of New England shut down and did not get back to normal for a week or so after the 'EDH'. Originally, the First Thirteen had celebrated the anniversary of the Mayflower's arrival in the New World in November 1620, this had become a colonial second 'harvest festival' imported from the old country and later a 'Thanksgiving Day' usually on the last Saturday in November each year. After 1776 there had been various festivities to gloat over the subjugation of the infamous rebellion, usually held around the end of August each year which had morphed into a traditional English late summer Bank Holiday. But then back in the 1870s somebody in Whitehall had had the bright idea of having a day of 'Imperial celebrations', the then King, Edward VII, had thought it was a marvellous idea and after a Royal Commission had sat and reviewed things Empire Day had been born, its first celebration occurring in 1881 after several years 'coming and going' over exactly when it ought to be celebrated.

The First Thirteen colonies of New England had acquired,

and maintained ever since, an influential, and periodically, powerful lobby in Westminster during the World War of 1857-65 and it had been a famous New England parliamentarian, Jefferson Wilson, who had laid the Private Member's Bill before the House of Commons proposing that Empire Day should henceforth be the first Sunday after 4th July unless that day was actually the Sabbath. In later years Wilson had courted no little controversy by plainly and repeatedly stating that his motive in making 4th July – the anniversary of the treachery of Philadelphia – Empire Day was no more or less than to 'rub the noses of recidivist republicans in the mire of 1776'.

On the East Coast the festivities went on until, as Abe's father used to say 'until they stopped' every year. In some colonies factories and whole towns literally shut down and the whole population went on vacation. Perhaps, half the people who would have flocked to the shores of the Upper Bay yesterday to enjoy the spectacle of the Fleet Review and to try to catch a glimpse of the King and Queen, would probably have been 'out-of-towners'.

On Long Island hotel and bed-and-breakfast proprietors eagerly rubbed their hands together for the coming of Empire Day which marked the end of the summer school term, and the real start of the holiday season which went on into the early autumn.

However, apart from thrilling the crowds at air shows the CAF tended to stay well and truly grounded during Empire Day Week. It was a standing joke in New England that if anybody wanted to invade then the day or two after Empire Day would be the best time; because probably, nobody would actually notice!

So, the question was: what were those fellows doing flying up and down the valley?

"It is supposed to be a holiday," Abe murmured, unable to shake off his uneasiness.

"What is it, husband?"

"Nothing. I guess I'm still a bit getting used to stuff," he apologised.

Kate was quiet, very serious.

"I know you've given up a lot for me."

Abe shook his head.

"I'd give up everything for you, wife."

She buried her face in his chest and he hugged her.

The breeze was blowing up the Mohawk valley from the south east, rustling the leaves overhead and carrying the roaring of aero engines in faint waves from far, far away, like waves crashing on a distant shore.

Chapter 35

New Brunswick, New Jersey

"Dad!"

After the excitement of recent days Henry Howland had determined to spend the day – which had dawned gloriously sunny – catching up with the garden chores he had neglected last week. The Colonial Security Service always paid well but frankly, lately some of the commissions he and his daughter, Jennifer, had been asked to undertake had been, to say the least, challenging.

He and Jennifer's dearly departed mother, Samantha, had first started working for Matthew Harrison about twenty years ago. The CSS had 'talent spotted' them, it seemed, after a Special Agent had attended the New Brunswick Players Christmas production of *A Winter's Tale* at the local playhouse. Jennifer had demonstrated a natural aptitude for 'the work' almost as soon as they had tested the waters of the 'surveillance and smoke and mirrors game'.

Usually, their work involved being anonymous, frequenting and listening, looking and occasionally spying on 'persons of interest' in public places, or impersonating this or that character. They were paid on a job by job basis, invariably in cash and if necessary, given ample time to prepare, to read themselves into their roles, and to rehearse. Occasionally, they were 'briefed' on the generalities, never the specifics, of a given CSS 'operation'. He and Samantha had never wanted to know anything they absolutely did not need to know. Jennifer was more curious but that was simply the consequence of her precocious youth.

Nonetheless, the last week had been something of a trial for them both.

Henry had been uncomfortable impersonating a police officer and told his employers as much. And as for actually attending that dreadful raid in the middle of the night in Gravesend. Goodness, the police had gone out of their way to wake up the whole street!

'What do you mean?' He had queried in alarm. 'I might be left alone with the suspect?"

"He's not violent and he'll be cuffed all the time.'

Both he and Jennifer had given each other odd looks when they finally got the interview scripts in the small hours of Saturday morning. It was one thing to ask them to distract everybody with a faux argument in a shopping mall or listen in a crowd as an agent provocateur stirred up trouble, or act as couriers across colony lines, or even to attend services or meetings where sedition might be talked but to actually conduct an interview in a police station!

'Just follow the script. We'll be just outside the door all the time.'

The CSS had put them up in a nice hotel at West Sayville last night after keeping them waiting around in Hempstead incommunicado all day yesterday so they had missed all the unpleasantness at the dockyard and out in the Upper Bay. That business at Wallabout Bay sounded bad enough but what had happened in the Upper Bay was a positive outrage...

"Dad!"

Henry had been on his knees weeding half-way down the garden, some twenty yards from the back door of the family's four-bedroom wood-framed house on Somerset Drive. Beyond the neat, pine-board fence at the bottom of the property one could always - whatever the time of year – see the masts of sail boats moored in the Raritan River. At this season there were always sails flapping, and elegant movements in the near distance.

Samantha had loved that view across to Middlesex County from whence she had hailed. They had met as student teachers at the old Cornwallis College – now long gone – and it had been if not love at first sight then the nearest thing to it!

"Daddy!"

Henry looked up, realising he had been wool gathering.

"That man that we interviewed at Hempstead has just been on the TV!"

The father staggered to his feet.

"Well, we knew he was suspected of being involved in..." He was going to say 'serious offences against the crown' before he was cut off.

"The CSS has just issued a statement saying he is suspected of being the guiding hand behind the disaster at the shipyard on Saturday afternoon, the attacks on the fleet yesterday and have asked the Director of Public Prosecutions to charge him with attempted Regicide!"

Henry had not seen his daughter this agitated since he could not remember when. She had been marvellously combative in the interview at Hempstead; her mother would have been proud of her. The way she carried off her performance was a thing of beauty...

"The CSS has arrested the poor man's whole family," the young woman told her father, her tone of voice indicating that she thought he was being more than usually hard of understanding. "His son-in-law was killed resisting arrest at the Admiralty Dockyard, his daughter is in hospital under heavy guard. They say one son worked on the speedboats that crashed into those big ships, and the other two might have tried to crash their aeroplanes into ships in the Bay. One of them is still alive. You'll never guess who was in the aeroplane with him?"

"This is true," her father confessed dryly. "I'll never guess!"

"Leonora Coolidge!"

"Who?" Henry Howland inquired patiently.

"The heiress, daddy!" Jennifer despaired of him. "Her

father owns practically all the Hamptons and three or four of the biggest hotels on Long Island! Those Coolidges!"

"Oh... What on earth was she doing in one of those aeroplanes?"

It seemed like a reasonable question.

The daughter shook her head in frustration.

"I should imagine that's what the CSS is asking her right now, daddy!"

"Yes, I should think so..." Henry Howland frowned. "You wouldn't have thought that chap was the sort, would you?"

"Isaac Fielding?" Jennifer paused for thought. "Well, the CSS are continually telling us that you can't tell that much about a book just from its cover."

Her father pursed his lips.

They had both read *Two Hundred Lost Years* from cover to cover as part of their preparation for the scene in the police station. All their assignments were 'scenes' or 'tableaus' of a theatrical nature, nothing to do with real life. That was what had been so unnerving about the last few days even before they heard about the tragic events elsewhere that weekend.

"No, but you can never tell. Can you?"

"Daddy!" Jennifer snapped angrily.

"What, my dear?"

"*That* man will be put on trial for his life."

"Quite right, he deserves whatever he gets..."

"You were at his house when he was arrested. You were in the car alone with him for over an hour. We both spent several hours with him or observing him on the day other members of his family tried to kill the King!"

"Oh," Henry Howland groaned, the penny dropping. "Oh, dear..."

"We could be called to give evidence at his trial!" This Jennifer impetuously said, out aloud, expressing what they were both thinking.

One way or another their career as well paid undercover – albeit dedicated thespian – undercover agents of the Colonial Security Service had just crashed into a brick wall.

Jennifer swallowed, dry-throated.

Her parents had been CSS informers most of her life, she had been one since she was a teenager and that had never been a problem.

Until now.

Now, everybody would soon know their dirty little secret!

Chapter 36

HMS Lion, Upper Bay

"What happened to the lady?" Alexander Fielding asked. He hurt everywhere. That was new, the pain had always been localised all the other times he had crashed. Not that he had been in much of a position to do anything about it; the battleship's 0.8-inch cannons had virtually chewed his Bristol V to pieces by the time it hit the water. He had no idea what had happened to the other aircraft. He assumed it must have been blown to smithereens.

"Your accomplice was only lightly injured. She was transferred ashore by police officers about an hour ago," a man with one of those English, stick-up-the-arse superior voices said dismissively as if he was addressing a dog turd.

"What do you mean," Alex protested feebly, 'my accomplice?"

Answer came there none.

"She was my bloody passenger, that's all..."

He must have passed out because the next time his eyes blinked open – not an easy thing because they seemed full of gunk – a stern-faced middle-aged woman in nursing apparel was standing over him taking his pulse.

Alex realised he had no idea where he was.

"You are in the sick bay of HMS Lion," the woman informed him. "The ship you tried to sink yesterday."

Whatever happened to the presumption of innocence?

Okay, so that was the way it was.

"The lady was okay?"

"Yes, cuts and bruises mainly. Unlike you, she was certified fit to be interrogated by the authorities on shore without delay."

"Anybody wants to talk to me I'm game," Alex insisted. "I've got nothing to hide. I tried to tip that idiot McIntyre into the sea. I would have if you hadn't shot off one of my wings."

He felt a beaker being pressed gently to his mouth, blissfully cool liquid wetting his cracked lips and trickling down his chin. Then he slept again.

"...I've got no time for traitors but if you badger this man I will have you thrown off the ship, do we understand each other Detective Inspector Danson?"

Alex would have sworn that the answering voice was feminine.

"I'm not here to 'badger' anybody, sir!"

She had brown eyes, a mane of red hair and she was watching him like a cat watches a mouse hole. Or at least that was the way it seemed to him.

The woman smiled wanly.

"This hasn't worked out very well for you, has it, Mister Fielding?"

She had a Vermont accent.

Alex tried to focus on the warrant card she held in front of his face.

Detective Inspector M.R.D. Danson.

"What does the 'M' stand for?"

It was not the most original chat-up line he had ever deployed; beggars could not be choosers.

"Melody," she explained. "My parents were musical. I'm not, probably because of all those piano lessons they forced me to attend when I was little."

Alex guessed she was in her mid-thirties.

No ring on her finger...

She was dressed like a Long Island middle-class housewife but had not bothered with any of the make-up too many women plastered over their faces these days.

Putting away her warrant card she sat in the chair at the foot of the bed and went on studying the injured man.

"You were a fighter ace in the Border War?"

"I shot down five Spanish scouts, if that's what you

mean?"

Melody Danson shrugged.

"Tough guy, yeah?"

Alex would have shrugged but it would have hurt too much.

"Okay," she sighed, drawing some kind of conclusion from the man in the cot's silence. "I'm here because Surgeon Commander Coverdale, this ship's chief doctor, is too English to tell me, a woman, to go to Hell. Just looking at you I know you are too badly knocked about for anything you say to me to be taken seriously in a court of law, even in the twin-colony. Not that this thing will go to court up here, the Governor will want to see justice done in Philadelphia. So, at least you'll get a fair trial before they hang you. I'm told that strictly speaking treason is still a hanging, drawing and quartering offence but I think Viscount De L'Isle will probably stop short of all that medieval nastiness."

"I'm not guilty of..."

"No, of course you're not, Mister Fielding," Melody Danson agreed. "But, when I tell you what you are up against you'll have to admit that things are not looking good for you."

Alex reckoned passing out again would be a good idea.

However, consciousness stubbornly persisted.

"This is the thing," the woman went on, matter of factly. "I'm only on the case because my colleagues were just about bright enough to work out that either they let me work my magic on Surgeon Commander Coverdale, or they would have to wait a week, or maybe two, to interview you and by that time the big boys in Philadelphia will be all over this one and their day or two in the spotlight will have come and gone before they even got the chance to get their dancing shoes on. So, the next person you talk to will be, I suspect, a jaundiced, somewhat embittered senior member of the

Colonial Security Service who once gave somebody the benefit of the doubt in nineteen-fifty-three and has been regretting it ever since."

The man said nothing.

"Your father, your brother William and when she gets out of hospital, if she lives..."

"Vicky's in hospital?"

"Yes, she lost her baby. They won't have told her that her husband is dead yet. They say he was in league with your father and together they conspired to blow up HMS Polyphemus as she was launched on Friday afternoon."

Alex must have been staring at her like a madman.

"Oh, you don't know about that?"

"I only flew down to Jamaica Bay on Friday evening. Sure, I heard about the accident, I flew over Wallabout Bay yesterday," he hesitated, "assuming this is Monday..."

She nodded.

"I didn't know it was sabotage..."

"John Watson was shot attempting to evade arrest by CSS officers." Melody Danson did not give this time to sink in. "The CSS are trying to establish if your brother Abraham was in one of the other aircraft involved in the suicide attacks on the big ships yesterday."

Alex tried to join up the pieces.

Nothing made sense.

Nothing except that he knew that Abe was nowhere near the Upper Bay at the time of the attack on the battleships. But if the CSS thought differently, then he was a marked man.

They had shot John Watson...

That guy was the straightest straight arrow he had ever met in his whole life!

But the CSS had shot him anyway...

They already had his father; and they had him, too.

If they were after Vicky as well this thing was insane,

hopeless.

They did not have Abe.

And if he had anything to do with it they were not going to get their hands on him any time soon!

Alex tried to speak.

No sound other than a hoarse croak passed his lips.

Melody Danson leaned over him.

"Abe didn't make it," Alex gasped, slipping back into the darkness.

"Sorry, say that again," the woman pleaded.

"Abe didn't make it…"

[The End]

Author's Endnote

'Empire Day' is the first book in the *New England Series* set in an alternative North America, two hundred years after the rebellion of the American colonies was crushed in 1776 when the Continental Army was destroyed at the battle of Long Island and its commander, George Washington was killed.

I hope you enjoyed it - or if you did not, sorry - but either way, thank you for reading and helping to keep the printed word alive. Remember, civilization depends on people like you.

———

Oh, please bear in mind that:

Inevitably, in writing an alternative history this book has referenced, attributed motives, actions and put words in the mouths of real, historical characters.

No motive, action or word attributed to a real person after 28th August 1776 actually happened or was said.

Whereas, to the best of my knowledge everything in this book which occurred before 28th August 1776 actually happened!

———

For details of all James Philip's published books and forthcoming publications can be found on his website www.jamesphilip.co.uk

Cover artwork concepts by James Philip
Graphic Design by Beastleigh Web Design

Printed in Great Britain
by Amazon